OPULENT OBSESSION

A DARK SECRET SOCIETY ROMANCE

ALTA HENSLEY

STASIA BLACK

Special Thank you to our editor, Maggie Ryan, and our wonderful beta readers.

And to our cover designer: Deranged Doctor.

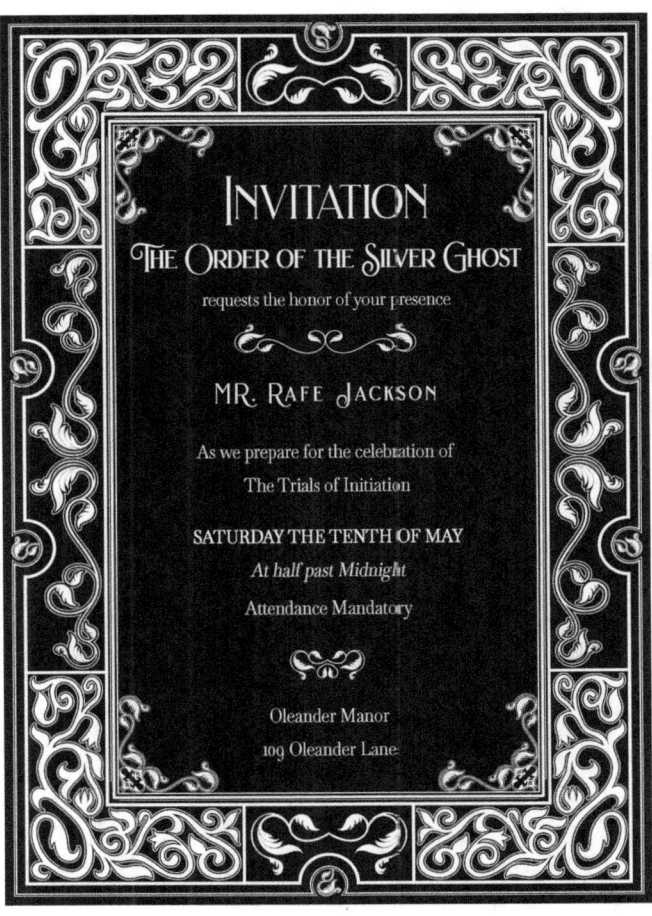

INVITATION

THE ORDER OF THE SILVER GHOST

requests the honor of your presence

MR. RAFE JACKSON

As we prepare for the celebration of
The Trials of Initiation

SATURDAY THE TENTH OF MAY

At half past Midnight

Attendance Mandatory

Oleander Manor
109 Oleander Lane

J ust because he was dead, didn't mean he was gone.

Haunted.

We were all haunted.

Timothy Jackson. All-star football star, valedictorian, first born, heir to the Jackson empire, my older brother by a year... and dead.

As I stood in my brother's room, staring at his shiny trophies, his awards framed and on display, and not a single speck of dust to be found, I realized how alive he truly was.

Frankly... more alive than I was.

Years had gone by, and the room hadn't changed one bit. I could still smell him, feel him, and practically hear his good-natured laugh. But no matter how hard I listened, I couldn't hear him answer my questions. When I most needed the ghost of my brother to haunt my ass, the bastard remained mute. I needed the answer...

How was I supposed to endure 109 days in the Oleander going through the Trials that were meant for *him* to complete?

I was the imposter, and yet, here I was with the invitation in my hand, and hours from beginning the Initiation. The Order of the Silver Ghost was his birthright, not mine. Firstborn, not the second —and often forgotten—Jackson son. But here I was, filling his shoes whether I wanted to or not. It was now my duty, my task, my curse.

"What are you doing in here?" my mother asked from behind me. Panic laced her words, and I knew she hated I was in *his* room.

I spun to face her, noticing how her eyes scanned every inch of space to see if I moved anything. God forbid I alter a single item. "I came by to say goodbye."

"Goodbye? Where are you going?"

"The Trials start tonight," I said with forced patience, trying to not snap at the woman who had nearly climbed into the same grave with her son and died with him. "I'll be out of contact for 109 days."

Her eyes seemed to fog over as she focused on a picture of Timothy after graduation in cap and gown. "That's right," she mumbled. "Your brother had always been excited for this day."

Yeah, I know.

"Remember how he would go to the Oleander with your father every chance he could?"

I nodded, remembering how I got to tag along most times even though I wasn't ever going to be a member of the Order. It's when I met my best friends. Even though they were all firstborn and would eventually go through their own Trials, they never treated me differently. I was one of them in all ways that mattered. Had any of us known sick fate would change all that for me, and indeed I would become one of them... well...

She walked over to Timothy's desk and touched a cup of pens and asked, "You didn't touch anything in here, did you? You didn't take anything, right?"

"I didn't move a thing," I said as I watched how she inspected every single item just to be certain it was exactly how it had been before he died.

Minus the dirty clothes that had been in the hamper, not a single item had been taken away or given to charity, or God forbid... given to his grieving brother as an item to remember him by. I had to sneak into his room to get that feeling of closeness. When I had asked for my brother's football jersey to remember him by, I still remember how it had nearly given my mother a stroke. Nothing... *nothing*, would leave this room.

She darted her eyes—drowning in disgust—to my arms that were fully covered in tattoos. I instantly regretted wearing a short-sleeve shirt. "I hope you plan to keep those covered. Your father would be embarrassed to have the Elders see all that... those markings all over you."

"I'll be wearing a tuxedo, Mom." I wanted to roll my eyes, but instead I leaned in and kissed her cheek which felt cool and lifeless. "I'll keep them covered. Don't worry."

"I don't know why you would do that to your body," she lectured for the hundredth time. "It makes no sense at all. Your brother didn't feel the need to destroy his skin."

Yeah, I know.

"And your hair." Her eyes, now full of judgment, moved to my head. "You really should have gotten a haircut before arriving tonight. It's shaggy and too long on top. You're representing the Jackson family, and... Timothy. You're representing him."

Yeah, I know.

I took a step toward the door, desperately needing to get out of my brother's tomb. My mother spun around and continued to scrutinize me.

"And that tattoo on your chest," she continued. "I can see it peeking out of your shirt. You really have to be careful and hide all that... ink."

There was a banner on my chest with the words: *Strength*, *Love*, and *Honor*. These were the words my brother and I would chant before something important. It was our motto. Our battle cry. And below those words on each pectoral was a sparrow with a compass right above their wings. My guide, my focus, and my way. It was ours, and now those words would forever be marked on my skin, and no matter how ashamed my mother was of that tattoo, it was the most important part of me. I would forever have Timothy on me, carved into my chest.

It was him.

It was me.

It was us.

Two brothers forever apart but hopefully someday we'd find our way back together again in the afterlife.

I nodded and gave the fakest smile I could muster. "Don't worry, Mom. I plan to keep my hair combed and slicked back, and all my tattoos will remain covered at all times. You have nothing to worry about. I'm not going to embarrass you or Dad."

Was I appeasing her? Did it make me sick to

my stomach as I did so? Was this the unhealthy and twisted way my mother and I communicated now? Would a therapist have a field day with this?

Yeah, I know.

I needed to change the subject because we were going down a deep, dark hole. Whenever my mother and I talked about Timothy, it would lead to her spending days in bed in a depression that no one could get her out of. It was my duty—just like it always was—to try to protect her from the painful memories. Even when I'd been just a senior in high school, and not equipped in the slightest to deal with a hysterical mother and a broken father, it had been my duty to be the strong one. Timothy was gone, and it all rested on my shoulders. So, I knew I needed to change the topic fast.

"Remember Fallon Perry," I began. "I saw her at Sully's party the other night. She's changed a lot. I barely recognized her."

My mother flinched as if she had just been punched. "That girl... Is she back in town?"

"It seemed that way," I said, uncertain why Fallon's name appeared to upset my mother so much. Fallon had practically grown up in our household. I'd never thought my mother had any ill will directed toward her. "She was working for the catering company that did the party. She looked really good."

My mother huffed. "Figures she would squander a perfectly good education. Everything was handed to that girl, and yet, here she is, wasting it by being some sort of waitress. Shame, but then again, she didn't exactly have a good role model as a mother."

"Her mother was nice," I said, though why I was trying to defend our old housekeeper, I didn't know. "Fallon was my best friend, Mom. I don't know why you're acting like she's some past enemy of ours or something. I thought you liked her."

She crossed her arms and walked over to my brother's bed, paused for several moments, and then ran her palm over his blue, flannel bedspread. "I never liked Fallon. Your father did. He pitied that girl for insane reasons."

I didn't like how she was speaking of Fallon, and my patience grew thin, even in Timothy's room which seemed to calm me when dealing with this woman. "Mom—"

"Let's just keep the past where it belongs," she cut in. "You have a lot on your plate right now. The last thing you need to do is to be thinking of that Fallon girl." She shrugged her shoulders as if she were shrugging away all the memories of a girl who didn't do anything to earn my mother's distaste. "She always wore too much black makeup around her eyes. And her hair. All that black. So much black."

"She was a teenager," I defended. "There were lots of goth girls back then. It's a normal phase."

"Phase? Like she had a reason to act out?" my mother snapped. "That girl was given opportunities. She was lucky to have the Jacksons treat her the way we did, and—"

"Let's drop this. I thought you would be interested to know that I had run into her. But it's not a big deal," I interrupted, trying to think of something else to discuss, because I could feel the tension growing in the room by the second.

"You need to focus. I don't think you truly grasp the importance of the Trials of Initiation," she said. "Your father is an Elder, and he had always hoped to hand down his business to Timothy. It was his dream, and the way it should have always been. You're the second son, and don't belong there."

Yeah, I know.

"But the Elders made an exception," she continued. "I hope you understand what a favor the Order is doing for this family. They're allowing your father's lineage to continue on, and it's up to you to honor your brother's memory in the best light. I don't want you going in there and messing this up. All eyes will be on you. They know it should be Timothy, and they'll be judging you against him."

Yeah, I know.

I loved my brother, but his memory was like poison in my blood. I was nothing but a shell of a man trying to fulfill my dead brother's destiny. That was who Rafe Jackson was.

That night my brother died in the car accident was the night I truly died right alongside him. I might as well have been a passenger. It wasn't just his life that was cut short. It was mine.

I died that night right along with the man I looked up to more than anyone else.

"I really should get going. I need to still shower and get dressed," I said, feeling like the walls of my brother's room were strangling me, and I couldn't escape fast enough.

My mother nodded, looking relieved that I was leaving the sanctuary she had created for my brother. It was sacred, and I didn't belong.

"I heard that Sully VanDoren failed the Trials," she said as she ushered me into the hallway.

"Yeah, but it seemed to work out for everyone in the end," I said, already knowing where this conversation was heading.

"I know you two are friends, but don't be like him. Be like that good boy Montgomery. Your father would be mortified if you screw this up.

We'd have to leave the Georgia social circle in shame if you do. Your father's business would never recover."

Yeah, I know.

"I plan to do this right, Mom. I'm not going to mess up. I promise you."

"It's just not fair," she said as she walked toward the top of the stairs with her eyes downcast and her shoulders slumped. "Timmy was made for this. Groomed to take over. He should be the one fighting for the silver cloak. Not you. It's just not fair."

Yeah, I know.

"Goodbye, Mom," I said under my breath, not that she was listening or even cared.

What was once a happy family was now shattered in a million pieces, and there was no way to fix what would be forever broken.

Timothy was gone.

I was here.

And now I had to walk in his shoes.

Strength, *Love*, and *Honor*.

2

FALLON

"Fallon! It's so good to see you, lassie!"

I set my black coffee on the table outside the cafe just in time to be enveloped in a giant, motherly hug by Mrs. Hawthorne. I'd always called her Mama H. We were on the middle of Main Street but it wasn't as if Mama H cared. She'd given up caring about what people said about her a long time ago, I suppose.

I hugged her back just as tightly. Fuck anyone who was looking on and tittering behind their hands. Yeah, the black sheep of the town was back. Let the gossipmongers run and tell whom they would.

Though in reality, likely no one would recognize me without my blue-black hair and goth make-up. I was perfectly respectable-looking these days.

In fact, likely no one was looking at us at all. It was just being back here made me fucking paranoid. It was the way they always made me feel here.

Other. Less than. Just the bastard kid of *the help*.

I gave Mama H one last squeeze and then pulled back. It was not hard to give her a genuine smile, no matter what my life had become lately. And I really meant it when I said, "It's so good to see you."

She smiled back at me, round and motherly, almost as much a mother to me as my own. Mom was always so busy cleaning other people's houses, and Mrs. H and Mom had been best friends for as long as I could remember. Mrs. H had been there for me when Mom was busy or when Mom had to work and couldn't come to my recitals or shows at Darlington Prep.

I was on scholarship, naturally. One of a few charity cases interspersed with all the rich, privileged kids.

I glanced past Mrs. H and shuddered a little at seeing Main Street. It was one of the few small towns in Georgia that was able to thrive without being a direct suburb of Atlanta. The men of Darlington had businesses that spanned the globe. Some had apartments in New York and abroad, but their home base was always here. Especially when an Initiate was going through the Trials.

The Order of the Silver Ghost was the town's worst-kept secret.

Everyone knew it existed, and a privileged few actually knew the name of the secret society, but there'd been whispers about what went on at the Oleander Mansion for as long as I could remember. Especially when Rafe and his friends got older, since all their fathers were involved.

Even thinking *his* name made me flinch.

I pulled back from Mama H and looked around at the elegant Main Street shops. The town thrived because of the men in the Order. After all, all those rich assholes and their wives liked to have fancy local digs to dine in and buy shit no one else in town could afford.

I shook my head. "God, I always swore once I got the hell out of this town, I was never coming back."

There weren't officially tracks to be on the wrong side of. Just a highway.

If you grew up on the wrong side of I-75, well then, you got to go to the shit public schools, and your parents likely worked at one of the shops that served the rich, took care of their kids... or, like my mom, cleaned their houses and all but wiped the shit from their asses.

Mrs. H nodded with understanding. "But here you are."

I looked at her deadpan. "Not by choice."

She smiled at that. "Oh, love, I'd give fair wages to bet it's circumstances, not choice, that land many a lassie in this town."

I frowned. What was that supposed to mean?

She waved a hand as if seeing and dismissing the question in my eyes. "Oh, thank you. Is that tea for me?"

I smiled and passed her the Earl Gray I knew she loved. "You haven't changed in all these years?"

She laughed. "I'm an institution, lass. Institutions don't change."

I scoffed at that. "You're only in your sixties. You're hardly growing cobwebs."

She just arched an eyebrow, then sat down and settled herself in the seat across the table from me. "Now tell me all about you. You went off and got yourself a fancy education all the way on the other coast! Sunny California!"

I grimaced. "A fancy education in a field no one seems to care about since I can't find a job."

Mrs. H nodded in concern. "Your mama said. I've heard it's hard out there for your generation.

And then you and your young man didn't work out either."

My man. I swallowed and looked down into my coffee.

It was spring in Darlington. There was still a chill in the air and the smell of recent rain. Everything was so shockingly familiar even after having been gone almost five years. I expected it all to be so different, to feel like a foreign country after all the changes I'd been through, after how I'd evolved and grown and—

I huffed out a breath. And yet the second I stepped back in town, I felt like the same little girl who'd run away all those years ago, betrayed and hurt beyond belief by the one person who I thought would always have my back—

"No, it didn't work out," I said, setting my coffee back down on the table harder than I'd meant to, sloshing a little over the side. I bit back a curse just in time. Mama H hated swearing, and I doubted me being a grown woman would stop her from smacking my wrist for it.

You and your young man. Her words echoed in my head. No, we hadn't worked out. We'd been close. I'd thought Jeoffrey was the one for me, for a time. He was a wonderful man. He was kind. He was stable. He'd tried to understand me. He'd asked me to marry him.

I'd been prepared to say *yes*. We'd talked about our future together.

We'd get a little place together in the Bay Area. He'd continue his law degree and I'd work on my studio art. It would be a beautiful life.

Except when he popped the question, what came out of my mouth?

NO.

No, I could not marry Jeoffrey Brown from San Francisco, California.

Because I was still stuck, my heart and my soul tangled in the heavy ivy and brambles of the deep South. I wasn't free to move forwards until I'd gone back. God how I hated it, but it was true.

I never completely understood it, but I was drawn back to this place as surely as a yoyo tied to a string. I just knew I wouldn't have any peace until I came back. A deep thorn had embedded itself in my heart here, and I'd never be free until I cut open the original wound and worked that shit out.

Then maybe I could heal. Then maybe I could finally be whole.

Dear God, please. Please, I want to be whole. I wanted more for my life than just walking around half-formed, being unable to really love anyone else, only half able to love myself. I was so tired of being angry at *everyone*, angry at my mother, angry at this town, at the world. Angry at God.

"You seem... unsettled, lassie."

I jerked my eyes up to meet Mrs. H's concerned ones. Shit. How could I have forgotten where I was and whom I was sitting with? She was always so attuned. Nothing ever got past her.

"I'm fine," I lied. "Just back for awhile after college. I thought I'd spend some time with Mom while I look for work. Everything's online these days so I figured I might as well hang out with her while I apply for jobs."

Mrs. H just nodded but didn't look at all convinced.

"Well, I know she's happier than a fox in a henhouse to have you back. And you're working for Mari's catering?"

"Yeah."

"I know she's happy to have you, but I've heard that woman does not keep light hours and expects the same of her employees."

That was putting it nicely. Mari was a slave driver. After every event, she expected the van cleaned out, all the dishes washed, the silverware sterilized, everything done just so. To be fair, she stayed until the very end, too. But it was exhausting work.

I'd thought coming home would mean some time off to think, reflect, and maybe do a little heal-ing. When in fact, it turned out to be non-stop work-till-I-drop manual labor. Between working with Mari and helping Mom clean out her old place and move into a smaller apartment, I went to bed exhausted every night.

It was in a nicer apartment complex, but still, it was an apartment. Always an apartment. Even after all this time, she didn't feel financially confident enough to afford a mortgage. A lifetime of cleaning people's toilets and for what? For *what*?

Mom had shared walls with neighbors her entire life. She always hated having to step quietly so she wouldn't make too much noise and have elderly Mrs. Toomey downstairs yell at her for it. Or being woken up by the neighbors we shared a wall with who couldn't grasp the idea of "quiet hours," blasting music and having parties at all hours when she was exhausted after her shift.

After a life of hard work, the woman deserved a little peace and quiet. But no, that wasn't how the world worked, was it? The men of some stupid secret Order practically lived in the huge manor while their other residences sat empty, and my mom broke her back her whole life—

Ugh, it was so infuriating. While I was away, the fury could stay at a low boil, but seeing Mom's delight at having an apartment with an in-unit laundry and thinking it was the height of luxury just pissed me off even more. She was excited about it being easier to do her own laundry after spending all day washing and folding *other people's* clothes.

I hated the way the stupid fucking world worked. It was backwards and fucked and I hated it. Mom thought it was ridiculous I refused to stay with her unless she allowed me to pay rent, but I know how hard she worked just to get the nicer apartment.

I'd always imagined that one day my art would take off, and I'd be able to buy my mom any house she wanted.

Then maybe you shouldn't have majored in Studio Art, idiot.

Yeah. I'd been regretting it lately. I of all people knew how frivolous it was to major in something so difficult to make real money at.

To be fair, I did minor in Accounting and almost did a double major. But my funding didn't allow for that, and I'd always been a slave to other people's whims as far as my education was concerned. So, fuck them, I was going to get the useless degree instead of the useful money-making one.

Uh, so yeah, I might not have the goth look anymore, but I never said I'd learned *quite* how to manage that annoying little rebellious streak in me.

"How's your mom, by the way?" Mama H looked at me over her cup of tea, her too observant eyes probably taking in far more than I wanted them to.

At least I could give another genuine smile. "Good. She's really good. She loves the new apartment. Though I swear she spends more time out on that tiny little back deck than she does in the house. She just sits out there and drinks coffee, swiping at the mosquitos, and reads on her eReader any time she's not at work."

I was still smiling as I lifted my coffee for a sip.

"You seen Rafe since you've been back?"

I choked on my coffee and set the cup down so roughly even more sloshed over the side onto the table than earlier. Jesus.

I swiped at the spill with my napkin and then glared at Mama H.

She knew the *R* subject was off-limits. He had been ever since I was driven out of this town in the middle of my senior year. I called to talk to both my mom and Mama H regularly but never, never, *never* did anyone involved bring up the accursed name of Rafe Jackson. Rafe, the boy who'd broken my heart and frankly, broken me.

I finished mopping up the coffee and mumbled, "I saw him the other day."

Never one to beat around the bush, Mrs. H asked, "How'd it go."

I glared up at her. "How do you think it went?"

She just raised an eyebrow slightly. "I don't know. That's why I'm asking."

My nostrils flared. She was really going to push this? "Fine. It went fine. I didn't throw the tray I was holding in his face or scream or cause a scene if that's what you're asking."

"That's not what I was asking," she said mildly. "I was wondering how it made you feel seeing him again after these years away."

I sagged back in my chair and threw my hands up in the air. "I don't know! I don't know how I felt!"

Except that wasn't true. Dear God. When I ran into Rafe at that celebratory reception for the girl getting back home from the hospital, I just froze for a second. Because even though he looked different —older, more filled out—he was still Rafe.

And I was still Fallon.

And we were just *us*.

He'd been my best friend since I was little. I wanted to run over and hug him. I wanted him to hug me back. I wanted to cling to him and beg him to never let me go.

And then I wanted to punch him in his stupid

fucking face for what he did to me. And yes, I wanted to scream at him and break things.

I wanted everything at once, and to run away, and it all *hurt*, and it felt good too, because any time I was in the presence of Rafe Jackson it felt better than the cold loneliness of not being in his presence and I—

"You know he's of age now." Mama H, already sitting close, leaned over so that her voice was right in my ear as she whispered, "He's about to go through his Initiation for the Order."

She pulled back and I had no clue what was on my face.

The Order.

Dear *God*. Rafe? Rafe was never supposed to go through the—

And then it sank in. Oh shit. Tim was gone. What the fuck, so they just moved on to the next in line? I blinked hard. Talk about *the heir and the spare*.

My heart squeezed in pain for Rafe. He'd always been little more than an extra, an afterthought, if even that, to his mother. She didn't give two shits about him when he was a kid, oh no, not when she had his Shining Golden Child older brother Timothy to fawn all over.

And now for Rafe to be pushed into taking Tim's place in the Initiation...

One night, Rafe told me what his friends talked about and this weird Initiation his older brother would have to go through as the eldest son. It seemed freaky as fuck, and I remember Rafe seeming so relieved it was nothing he'd ever have to do.

My throat went dry as it hit me all over again. Timothy was gone. Now Rafe *was* the eldest son. Oh Rafe. How could I want to comfort him and still want to slug him in the face all at the same time?

I swallowed again. "Is... is he okay?"

Mama H's face softened. "Aye, the lad will do all right. Montgomery's there to watch over him."

I nodded. Montgomery had always been a bit stuffy but a good enough guy. He'd never been anything but nice to me, and for a Darlington Prep student, that said a lot.

As a poor kid on scholarship, most of the guys treated me like I'd been put on their campus as free, no-consequence pussy. Then they got pissy when I wouldn't put out. Small wonder I dyed my hair black, wore goth make-up and embraced a perpetual Come-Near-Me-and-I'll-Fuck-You-Up vibe. I was in fucking survival mode.

Rafe's friends were the rare exception to the rule, I do remember that. And really, I'd had no idea just how bad high school could be. Rafe and Montgomery and the rest of them had probably shielded me far more than I ever knew. Even just being associated with them at all had likely been protection.

"Lass, can we take our drinks to go? Maybe you'll take an old woman for a walk? It'd be good for these stiff joints."

I jolted from my thoughts and gave her a look. "You know you're a spry one, Mama H. You can't fool me."

She laughed, her eyes glinting as she gave me a wink. "Shhh, don't give away my secrets. People expect less of an old woman. They forget I can still scheme."

I tugged my purse on my shoulder and grabbed my coffee, pushing out my chair. "Okay, but where are we going?"

Mama H looked around and I saw that there were a couple pairs of eyes on us after all. Mama H kept her head high but cut her eyes to me. "Somewhere we can talk without any prying eyes or ears. It's time you learned the truth about how me and your mama met."

I frowned at her. "You met when she moved here."

"Baby girl, didn't you ever ask yourself *why* she ended up in Darlington? Or me, for that matter?"

I opened my mouth, ready to give an answer, before I realized I didn't have one. Wait a second, why the hell had Mom come here? How had I never really asked more about it? I mean, Mom just always said she grew up in a broken home and she never wanted to talk about it. She always said her life started when I was born. It was sweet, even if I'd always suspected it was a cop-out.

Other than that, all I knew was that she and Mama H had become best friends while Mom was pregnant with me. Mama H had helped her find work—work cleaning Rafe's family house.

I was bitter about it but at the same time, those years were some of the best of my life. Because I'd had Rafe.

I was five years old and was supposed to be coloring in the laundry room while Mom went and washed the upstairs toilets. But I'd gotten bored. I didn't like being cooped up. Hated it, in fact. But our neighbor Miss Reyes hadn't been able to watch me that day—and I was glad to escape the old lady. She smelled funny and only wanted to watch Spanish soap operas all day.

I'd been excited to come with my mom. Until I realized it meant sitting in a laundry room all day being quiet as a mouse because there was a mean dragon lady who yelled at Mommy if either of us made too much noise. I'd only been there two times before.

Yes, the laundry room did smell nice, and it was

fun when Mommy let me help her fold the clothes. She said I was the bestest helper and she promised that later she'd teach me how to fold the fluffy towels.

But she wasn't coming back downstairs, and I was bored.

I knew it was naughty, but I was a *very* quiet mouse, and I was hungry. Mice snuck around to get food without anyone noticing, right? So, I wasn't *technically* breaking the rules, because Mommy had told me to be like a mouse.

It seemed like foolproof logic at the time.

So, eveeeeeeeeeeer so slowly, I pushed the door to the laundry room open, wincing when it squeaked, and then, quick as I could, in just my socks so I would barely make a sound, I pranced down the little hallway to where the kitchen was.

I remembered because Mommy had let me be in there with her while she cooked dinner for the dragon lady and her family one time. Only because no one was home and she was making cookies for the dragon lady's kids, and Mommy knew how much I loved making cookies.

I knew my way to the kitchen, and I scurried on my little mouse feet. I'd climbed onto the counter and was just reaching up into the cabinet where I knew the graham crackers were stored—the name-brand kind and not the kind Mommy had at home that tasted a little like cardboard. No, these were the good kind where you could almost taste the honey. I'd just reached my little hand in the box, just like a mouse, when—

"Who're you?" a voice demanded.

I spun around on the counter so fast I almost fell. I was terrified and my heart beat so fast. Oh no! The dragon lady was going to catch me! Mama would be so mad!

But then I saw it was just a little boy.

He wasn't any bigger than me, so I stuck my tongue out at him. "What do you care? I'm nobody." And then I shoved a handful of graham cracker animals into my mouth.

"Hey!" he said. "Those are mine!"

I frowned, my hand already back in the box. "Yours?" I asked, mouth full of crumbs.

He puffed out his chest. "Yeah, they're mine. I live here. You're the thief. You better tell me who you are or I'll call the cops on you."

Oh no! Mommy would *really* be mad if this stupid boy called the *cops* on me. I hadn't meant to steal, I was just hungry. And Mommy had let me eat a few of the crackers when we'd made cookies and—

I jumped down from the counter and hurled myself at the little boy. "Take it back! Take it back. You better not call anybody or I'll— I'll—"

"Get off me!" he screeched, wrestling underneath me but unable to throw me off. I wasn't an idiot. If I let him go, he'd go tell on me.

Then again, his screeching and caterwauling were starting to get mighty loud.

"Stop it!" I hissed, trying to cover his mouth with my hand. "Shut up. Stop crying!"

That stopped him. He looked offended like I'd just hit him. "I'm not *crying*. Boys don't cry."

Well, I knew that wasn't true. There was a boy in the apartment building who cried all the time. I always heard him through the walls. And there was that other boy, stupid Matthew, who'd been mean to me, and then I'd hit him, and *he'd* cried.

"Boys do so cry. I can make *you* cry."

He jutted out his chin. "Cannot."

"Can too."

"Cannot."

"Can too." Then I punched him in the stomach. Not very hard. Just enough that I thought it would make him cry.

But he was right. He just stayed there on the floor and blinked at me, chin still out, blinking at me and obviously determined not to give in even though a sheen of water covered his eyes.

I thought it'd be mean to hit him again, so I moved off him and held out my hand. I respected anyone who could take one of my punches and not cry. "I'm Fallon. Wanna be friends?"

It was like I'd just offered him a plate of chocolate chip peanut butter cookies, his face lit up so big and bright. "Sure. I'm Rafe Jackson."

I frowned. *Jackson.* That was the same name as the dragon lady. She was Mrs. Jackson, that was what Mommy said I was supposed to call her if I ever saw her.

But my friend Renata, who was Miss Reyes' granddaughter—she had a bad daddy who was in jail, and she was still nice. So maybe Rafe could still be nice and be my friend even if his mom was a mean dragon lady.

So, I shook his hand and decided right there and then, "Okay, we'll be best friends." Then I looked him over a little closer. Actually, I'd never had any friends who were boys. So, I nodded and added, "And when we grow up, we can get married."

He shrugged. Then we took the box of graham cracker animals outside, and he showed me all the best spots for hide and seek, which his older brother was always too busy to play with him.

God, I blinked a few times, coming out of the memory. I hadn't thought about how Rafe and I had met in years. I pushed some hair behind my ear, again feeling that strange sense of déjà vu I'd been having ever since I'd driven into town two months ago. I didn't like it. No, I didn't like it one bit.

"So," Mama H prompted. "Didn't you ever wonder?"

"What?" I looked over at her, still feeling disoriented from thinking about the past. Then I remembered she'd been asking about Mom and that was what had taken me back. I shook my head. "No, no, I guess I never knew why Mom landed here. She was always vague about her past before I was born."

Mama H, now standing alongside me, looked around like she was again making sure no one else was in hearing distance. When she was satisfied no one was close, she leaned in one more time. "Oh, lass, we were both belles presented to the Initiates of the Order. Different years, mind you, but we bonded because we were both *not* chosen by our respective Initiates. We were the leftovers. The rejects. Over the years, some of us have become something of a club."

My mouth dropped open as tidbits of what Rafe had told me back in the day filtered through my head. Wait... WHAT?

My mom and Mama H had been... rejected belles? Like the same ones who went to all the... the sex parties. I remembered what Rafe had furtively described to me. Once he and his friends had snuck onto the Oleander grounds during a Trial and peeked in the ballroom window. He'd blushed when I demanded he tell me what he'd seen. I'd had to put his arm in a wrestling lock until he said uncle and finally gave up the info.

He said they'd seen a bunch of naked women fucking a roomful of men. He'd been a little more delicate about it, but that was the gist. He'd definitely described a group orgy, though. And then he'd gotten really freaked out and said they'd kill him if they knew he'd ever told, and I had to *swear* to never tell, and I never had.

But now here was Mama H telling she'd been one of those women at some point. And... and so had my... *mother*?

"Come with me, lassie," Mama H said calmly. "You'll catch a bug with your mouth open like that. We'll find a good place to chat."

I somehow managed a nod, and she took my arm and steered me out from amidst the cafe tables and down the street.

3

RAFE

W hite.

Why was the ballroom that hosted such dark and depraved acts white?

And to top it off, all the recruits—including myself—wore a white tuxedo. Were we all cloaking the black of the sin in the white of our elegant attire? White should symbolize purity, and we were far from angelic and innocent here at the Oleander Manor.

And the Elders in their silver cloaks flooded the room, staring on with their judgmental eyes. They watched us. They watched me.

The Order of the Silver Ghost always watched me. Even when all eyes weren't on me, I could still feel them. I could still hear their thoughts.

I did not belong.

Timothy should be here in the white tux. He should be the one to go through the Trials of Initiation and earn his membership to the Order. He should be the one to inherit my family's oil company. Not me. They knew it. I knew it. Every single person in this room knew it.

I would always be the imposter.

"Are you ready for the Trials to begin?" Beau Radcliffe asked as he walked up to where I stood and patted my back. "I'm next in line, and I can tell you one thing... I don't think I'll be ready for this. If Sully failed it, then who's to say we can pass this?"

"We both *want* to be a member of the Order. That's the big difference."

"Do we?" Beau mumbled as he took a sip of his drink, looking around the ballroom at all the members and all the Elders. "I understand why you do," he added. "You've always tried to live up to his memory. You've been trying to live up to your father's expectations too. I mean... I get it. I do. The Southern Gentleman curse is strong in all of us."

I had been helping run my father's business since high school. I had skipped college because what was the point in studying for anything but the world of oil? My career was set in stone the minute my brother died. The business was going to be mine, so what better education but to dive right in and learn every inch of the biz from good ol' Pops. Did I want the job?

Did it matter?

Looking down at my scotch, I couldn't decide if I should down it in one swallow or to not drink it at all. I knew I needed liquid courage, but my stomach twisted in knots as the large grandfather clock that mastered the ballroom ticked away. The hands of the face were golden sabers with tiny rubies, and there was no way to not stare as my time grew near.

The belles would be presented to us soon enough. We were all gathered and ready, and it was just a matter of minutes before they would begin the ceremony.

"You're going to be okay," Montgomery said as he walked up and stood next to Beau and me. Though he was my friend, he was now... different as he stood with his silver robe and the smell of *member* permeating from his Order energy. "I know this is intense. It wasn't easy for me, and it wasn't easy for Sully, but I want you to know you can do this."

He looked at me closely, examining my face. "I also want you to know I don't condone the shit they're going to make you go through. I hate this. I do. I hate these Trials; I hate having to witness everything that happens. I'll try my best to be there for you, but I also don't want to fuck up your chances by getting involved."

"How's your fianceé feel about you attending all the fuck parties?" Beau asked as he finished off his drink in one big swallow and placed his glass down on a table to our right. "I can't imagine Grace is happy that you attend all these."

"She fucking hates it," Montgomery answered without hesitation. "She hates the Order but understands why I want to be part of it. It's my world, and she has accepted that. It's our heritage and runs in our veins. But she also knows my cock belongs to only her, and she trusts my ass."

He took a drink, glancing around at the other members who mingled as if it were just any ordinary cocktail party they were attending. "Somewhere along the line, the Order changed. It's not the same as it was back when we were boys. I know I've said this, but I want to change it into something better again. Something better than it ever was. I have a bigger goal. A long-term goal in mind."

He looked around at all of us. "But I can't do this alone. I need you guys to become members. We need new blood that isn't fucked up and tainted with Viagra and overpriced bourbon. We aren't the only recruits coming in. The next batch will be soon after us and will have to endure the same shit unless we stop it. I truly don't believe our great-great-grandfathers would have condoned some of this crap."

Montgomery's words sounded nice, but I didn't exactly have such lofty goals. I was just trying to survive the night here. I scanned the room looking for my dad. I didn't expect for him to approach me tonight as I was a lowly recruit and he was an Elder, but it still would have been nice to get his encouragement even in the smallest amount.

Instead, he stood with drink in hand, a large smile on his face, as he laughed during a conversation with Walker's dad, looking without a care in the world. It wasn't like his only living son was about to dance with the devil tonight and maybe needed his father. No, that wasn't the way it was done in the Order.

I swallowed my emotions along with my swallow of scotch.

Emmett and Walker approached us in their white tuxedos. It was a reminder that we were the outsiders. We were the cluster of recruits in line to claim our membership. We were nothing but blank, invisible, white ghosts until we became members of the Order.

"Seems weird being here without Sully," Walker said. "Miss the asshole," he added with a smirk.

"Why did he fail?" Emmett asked Montgomery.

Montgomery seemed uncomfortable with the question. "I'm trying to be a good friend to you guys, but there are rules about what the recruits can and can't know. Eventually you'll all know the answers"—his eyes darted around the room—"but I can't discuss that. Especially here."

"Do you think I have a chance of actually passing it?" I asked, wondering if I was cut out for this.

It wasn't like the inherited malice was in my bones. I was the secondborn. The ghosts who haunted the Oleander Manor could very well have other ideas for me. They knew the truth. They knew it should be Timothy here in the white tux. A small, superstitious part of me was terrified that they were the true judges of an Initiate's worth.

Montgomery reached out and patted my arm. "You got this. Just do what's asked of you even though your morals will be screaming at you not to. Pick a belle who you feel you can endure the 109 days with. It's long. It's brutal. It's extremely boring at times as day after day blend together. And you're gonna have to fuck the belle. A lot. No way around that. So, make sure the girl gets your cock hard. Otherwise, you're going to really regret it."

My friends laughed, but I didn't. I wasn't in the mood to do anything but wait. Wait...

The loud hammer strike of twelve chimes echoed in the room. Canes being held by the Elders matched the cadence and the intensity as they banged against the white marble floor. The Choosing of the Belles was about to begin.

"Bring in the belles," one of the Elders demanded after the twelfth punch of his cane.

The recruits lined up with me in the center of the room. We stood at attention and waited.

We had done this before. Once for Montgomery, and once for Sully. Eventually there would only be one standing here from our cluster. I suppose I was happy that I wasn't the last one. At least I had moral support on each side of me as Emmett, Walker, and Beau flanked me in the repeated ritual.

I'd tried to prepare myself for this moment. I'd told myself I'd just pick one of the passingly pretty ones—not a beautiful one who'd probably be too needy or high-maintenance, and not one of the dull-looking ones. Like Montgomery said, I needed at least a passing attraction to the girl.

The room went silent, and I waited for the sound of heels—the belles were coming but instead of being a spectator like the times before, I knew this time it was my turn.

Twenty young women.

The Order of the Silver Ghost deemed the

number centuries ago, just as they decided exactly what would happen step by step of every moment of not only tonight but of the next 109 days. I was at their mercy, and the innocent, and unfortunate, belle was as well.

I felt bad for the women. I hated that I had to choose one to endure this hell with me. I knew they wanted to be chosen, but they had no idea what that truly meant. Not really. They didn't know they were caught in a fire and the only way to make it out without burns was to run away tonight.

I could save nineteen of them from the flames, but one was doomed to burn alive with me.

As they entered the room, they stood in a line before us. I knew I was to study each one. Pick the hottest, or at the very least the most interesting. But the truth of the matter was they all would be pretty. I hadn't seen a belle yet who wasn't.

Long flowing ball gowns moved before me. Tiny, corseted frames, massive amounts of fabrics, utmost beauty and—

What the fuck! Was this some kind of sick joke?

Fallon Perry?

What the fuck was she doing here?

I blinked several times in hopes that I wasn't seeing the same woman whom I had reconnected —even briefly—with at Sully's party. I looked around, waiting for Montgomery to laugh and say it was a sick prank and to bring out the real girls now.

But no one was laughing, and no one was moving and Fallon fucking *Perry* stood in front of me as one of the Belles of the Midnight Ball. I shook my head. Maybe it was just some chick who *looked* like her. Because why the hell would Fallon be one of the belles? This couldn't be right.

I'd only had one swallow of scotch and I didn't feel dizzy or high. I hadn't been drugged. Still, I couldn't help wondering if I was just imagining the one woman who had ever given me comfort in my life, a sudden apparition to help me get through this night?

But the longer I stared, the more certain I became.

It was Fallon. My Fallon.

There she stood—the only one dressed in violet—who made brief eye contact with me before she looked down to the ground as if ashamed.

Heat fired through my blood. She should be ashamed! What the hell was she doing here?

She knew better than this! She knew well enough about the Order and what that meant. She wasn't stupid. So why the fuck was she here?

Her dark eyes lifted but instead of looking at me, she studied her surroundings. She soaked in the nightmare of this morbid Cinderella ball.

Yes, Fallon, the stories were true.

Yes, this is real.

Yes, you should get the hell out of here right now.

"Display the belles," the Elder demanded with a beat of the cane.

I needed to get her out of here. This was insanity. The last girl—Montgomery might not be willing to spill secrets, but Sully had taken me aside last week and told me the hell they put the "belles" through. They'd buried his girlfriend alive when she was a belle. Sweet little Portia!

My guts rebelled at the thought of anyone ever putting hands on Fallon like that. She didn't belong here. I'd never let these fuckers lay one finger on her.

But I couldn't take one step towards her. I couldn't grab her around the waist, hike her over my shoulder, and march her out of the mansion like I wanted. There were invisible ghostly shackles holding me in place. My being here was about more than me. I was fulfilling my brother's legacy. I couldn't just— I couldn't just—

I glanced at my father to see if he noticed Fallon was one of the belles. If he did, he didn't show it on his face. He stood expressionless as he waited for the ceremony to continue.

Remember my best friend from childhood, Dad? Remember Fallon Perry? Remember the little girl who grew up in our house? Remember her? Well, she's here in the Oleander! Aren't you going to stop it?

Of course not.

Another Elder began the procession of the belles by leading them single file through the ballroom. He walked them in front of the cloaked Elders first, then the members, and finally to us. This is what was done every single time and no surprise. Yet, it didn't seem real. I wasn't sure if it was because this was all done for my benefit or because Fallon fucking Perry was one of the belles.

They repeated the act three times, circling the room with the sound of their expensive shoes tapping against the white floor. I couldn't focus on a single belle other than Fallon. Her dark hair hung in curls down her back. Her makeup, though much less and lighter than when we were friends in high school, still remained smoky around the green color of her eyes. She held her head proud, her shoulders back in confidence, and her body broke through the thick air of evil as the only light and good in the room.

But she shouldn't be here.

God, what was she doing here?

The twenty belles all came from a place of poverty. There was no secret each one of them was here for money. The Order promised them their dreams. Whatever it was they wanted would be theirs if chosen. If the belle completed the Trials, then all would be at their fingertips.

But Fallon?

No, she didn't exactly have money. I wouldn't have considered her poor or in need. Or was she? It wasn't like I knew what happened to her after she left during our senior year. Come to think of it, her mother stopped being our housekeeper at the same time and well... we had lost touch. So, I guess it was fair to say that I didn't exactly know the circumstances that had brought her here.

But regardless, if she needed money... well, I had plenty to give. I may not have the same power or money as my father, but I was definitely well off, and...

She wasn't like these other belles.

She may not be the rich socialite, or even the southern debutante like the wealthy women in my world. But still...

She was Fallon.

My Fallon.

"Rafe Jackson," the Elder called out as the belles lined up once again before me and the recruits who hadn't moved an inch even though I fought the urge to run to Fallon. "It is time for you to choose the belle."

The Elder who had been leading the procession of belles walked over to where I stood and opened his fist. Resting on his palm was a black satin ribbon. I already knew what to do next as I had watched both of my friends do this before me.

Taking the ribbon, I took a deep inhale and began the touching of the pearls. I had to keep moving. I couldn't raise the issue. I couldn't let on that I knew one of the belles. I wasn't sure what would occur if the Elders were made aware of that fact. I couldn't stop the ritual before it truly had begun.

Don't make eye contact with Fallon.

Ignore her.

One by one, I approached each female and briefly touched the pearl necklace they all wore. I hadn't reached Fallon yet but knew she was coming soon.

Going through the motions, steadying my nerves, and focusing on the ceremonial act was all I could do. Thinking about her would mess this all up. All eyes were on me. I knew this. I wasn't going to let my father down or my brother. Timothy would have wanted me to do this right. Nothing and *no-one* could screw this up for me.

Focus on the task at hand—following the steps of Montgomery and Sully before me, I would conduct the ceremony perfectly.

And then I reached Fallon.

She locked eyes with me as I reached out to

caress her necklace. I wanted to talk to her. I wanted to hold her, hide her, run away with her. I wanted to yell and scream at her. I wanted... I needed to keep moving on. No way was I going to choose her.

It was my duty to protect her even if she hated me for it.

No way would I allow her to go through the steps of the Initiation with me. I didn't know exactly what would occur, but I had heard enough from Montgomery and Sully, not to mention the years of rumors, to know this manor was not a place for her. If I chose her... I would have to stand back and watch her suffer.

I would never allow that to happen.

So even if she wanted me to choose her. Even if she expected me to choose her...

The answer was no.

I moved to the next belle who wore a lovely yellow dress. Yes, the girl in yellow would have to do.

Looking down to the string of white pearls resting against her freckled flesh, I yanked hard. The necklace broke from her neck and the tiny pearls scattered around the floor. Her eyes widened, tears formed, and her lips trembled, but she remained in place.

Breaking the necklace. An act to show just how

easy it is for The Order of the Silver Ghost to give you riches only to take them away. *What you believe to be yours can be ruined with such ease.* We had recited this motto over and over as boys. I knew exactly how easy it was for the Order to control everything we did. They could destroy me. They could destroy my father. They could destroy Fallon. And I wasn't about to let that happen.

Not wasting any time and trying to not feel the glare of Fallon beside me, I replaced the pearls that had been on the yellow-dressed belle's neck with the black ribbon. I needed Fallon and the rest of the belles to leave immediately, and the faster I tied the ribbon around the now shaking belle, the better.

"Rafe Jackson, have you chosen your belle for the Initiation?"

I took a step back from the belle in yellow and glanced at Fallon, who looked at me as if I had just stabbed a dagger through her heart.

I'm sorry, Fallon. So sorry.

But no way am I going to allow you to be a belle to be broken.

"I have chosen," I stated firmly. "I have chosen my belle."

W hat the fuck had just happened?

Mrs. Hawthorne told me that if I accepted the invitation, I'd be a shoo-in. After we'd gone for our walk, and she'd finally told me everything—and I mean *everything*, at least everything she knew—she brought up the craziest idea of all. She'd given me the invitation to be a belle myself.

She said it was perfect. That I could be a belle, and unlike my mother, I'd be chosen. That Rafe would pick me and I could finally have all the desires of my heart—all that I frankly *deserved*. It was the perfect solution. I'd be able to take care of Mom. I'd get what had always been due me, what had been stolen from her so long ago.

But Rafe had ruined everything.

He'd gone and fucking *humiliated* me. Again,

rejecting me. And this time not just in a little written note telling me he was sorry that I had such strong feelings for him, but sorry he didn't feel the same way. Oh God, that note. Cause he hadn't stopped there. No, he'd gone on and said he didn't think even being long-distance friends was such a good idea anymore because he felt bad leading me on, but thanks for the ride and here's a $100 for the road.

His brother had just died, and I'd tried giving him the benefit of the doubt. He'd never been so cold to me in the entirety of our over-a-decade-long friendship, and he'd certainly never just outright given me money like that.

It had made me feel... cheap. Like he was distilling our friendship down to a transaction. *I'm tired of you, please go away, here's a hundred bucks if that will make it happen faster.*

But I'd been stubborn. I wasn't going to give up on ten years of being best friends, especially when I thought he might need me—Timothy had just *died* for Christ's sake. If it had been *my* sibling, all I would have wanted was to bury my cheek against his broad, comforting chest.

However, when I went by, his mother answered the door and said he didn't want to see me. He'd asked her to be his gatekeeper after the note so that he didn't even have to deal with me.

And then everything moved so quickly. I was accepted into the prestigious Art Center College of Design in Pasadena, California. I had to go. My scholarship at Darlington had dried up. My mysterious benefactor fueling my Darlington Scholarship had decided to stop paying my way.

I had no choice but to go.

I suppose it wasn't true. I could have stayed and finished out my education in the shit public school system. I would have, if there'd been even a whisper or whimper of encouragement from Rafe.

But all I got was the cold stone of his walkway and the silence of the door being shut repeatedly in my face by his mother. His email went unchecked. No word. No communication.

Thirteen years of friendship and—well, I'd hoped for more. But then I'd always been a fool for imagining there could be anything between us, him the prince and me, the help's daughter—and then he'd just cut me from his life as easily as the trash my mother threw out each week.

And so, ten days later, I'd boarded a bus, and never came home.

Until now.

For what? For this? Only to make myself as beautiful and appealing as a slutty cupcake, give him my soul through my eyes, and be rejected as thoroughly and painfully as when we were stupid kids?

Fuck Mrs. Hawthorne for ever helping to get my hopes up. I couldn't believe I even came here to the Oleander. I couldn't *believe* I was repeating my mother's fate.

I was a rejected belle now, too. I guess I could join their little club.

I was shocked when Mama H told me. Was it really only yesterday that she blew my world wide open? Just yesterday when I followed her from the cafe to the little picturesque park by the river where she told me a tale I'll never forget?

"Your mother was young and desperate when she got to this town," Mama H said as she sat down on a park bench along an empty path. It was 11am on a Friday and no one was around. Swallowing hard, I sat down beside her. Did I want to hear what she had to say? Even then I knew that whatever Mama H was about to tell me, it was big. Maybe even rock-my-foundation big.

She didn't disappoint. "She always reminded me a lot of myself. She worked as a washerwoman at one of the motels in a nearby town when she got the invitation."

"Invitation?"

"To compete as a belle for the attention of one of the Initiates in the Order of the Silver Ghost."

My head snapped to look at her. She wasn't looking at me. She still stared straight ahead. Even though her demeanor was calm, I knew better. She was spilling secrets that were sacred. Secrets that powerful men would go to extreme lengths to be kept quiet.

"Why are you telling me this?"

Finally, Mama H looked my way. Her eyes were direct. She was unafraid. "You deserve to know. It's your heritage."

I'd felt my brow furrow. What the hell did *that* mean?

But she was already barreling on. "The Invitation could have meant everything to your mother. A new life. Riches beyond anything she'd ever known. All her dreams come true."

I shook my head, confused. We both knew that wasn't what happened.

Mama H's face softened. "She wasn't chosen that night."

I felt her words like a physical blow. Not because I cared that much, but because I could imagine the blow my mother had felt. All her hopes for a better future, snatched away simply because a man hadn't chosen her.

So, if she *hadn't* been chosen, why the hell was Mama H even telling me this story?

"She was among the rejects," Mama H went on.

Well, that felt like a harsh way to put it, sheesh, but then she continued, "—just like I was."

My mouth dropped open just like when she'd first said it minutes before. I could barely voice the next words, "I don't understand. I can't imagine you as—"

She laughed heartily. "I wasn't always the woman you see before you. In my youth, I was quite the looker."

I frowned. I'd always thought Mama H beautiful, but in the motherly, comforting way of rounded, soft older woman. I tried to peer through that and reverse the years, and yes, just *there*, I could see it, the winking, mischievous young woman, hungry for life and adventure.

"What—" I stopped myself right before I asked, *What happened?* That seemed rude and offensive to ask, even though it was what I really wanted to know.

Mama H looked back out across the river. "I was barely of age when I made my way to this country. My father brought me over on a business trip. Of course he did."

Her face went dark. "I was his favorite daughter to rape every night, so naturally he couldn't leave me behind for even a day."

I blanched. "Mama H—" I reached out a hand

and she caught it by my wrist, then settled it gently back on my own lap.

"I've dealt with that evil man, lass, don't you worry. He doesn't walk this earth anymore."

Now my eyes were as wide as my open mouth. I snapped it shut. Holy shit. Mama H had secret depths I never could have guessed.

And she was just laying them all bare to me for some reason, because she went on.

"I ran away from him and disappeared as best I knew. It was a little easier to do back then. No cell phones or GPS trackers and all that nonsense. I rode a bus south and then got off at a random stop and walked down the most deserted road I could. Eventually I found my way up a long, winding drive with beautiful oak trees lining both sides, to the most beautiful mansion I'd ever seen. It was something out of a storybook."

Even now, all these years later, her voice took on a wistful quality as she spoke. "I'd lived in the city my whole life. A dirty part of Glasgow, and Glasgow's already ranked the dirtiest city in all of Scotland. But here everything was so pristine and beautiful and smelled of pines and fresh air." She closed her eyes and inhaled, a peaceful smile overcoming her face.

"When I knocked on the door, they asked if I was one of the belles. I'd gotten there just in time for an Initiate's ball. The harried woman just let me in without even asking to see my invitation." Mama H shook her head. "It was an unorganized chaos with the belles back then. It's a wonder they got *anything* accomplished."

I smiled even as I wanted to push her to hurry up the story. What happened next? How did she meet my mom? But if there was one thing I'd learned in all my time with Mama H, it was that you never rushed her.

Still, I couldn't help asking. "So, what'd you do?" I'd only heard whispered tidbits about the "belles" and what supposedly happened during these "Initiations". Rafe used to speculate about the stuff his brother would have to do one day when he went through the Trials, but it was always this esoteric, far-away thing. Like the formalities or activities of a royal family, it was so far away from our lives.

A wicked glint came into Mama H's eyes. "I took advantage of the disarray. I found a spare dress and made myself up like one of the belles."

Well, she'd managed to shock me again. My mouth dropped open once more. "You pretended to be one?"

She shrugged haughtily. "After asking around, I realized they were all women like me. We all had sad stories, and I'd stumbled upon a real-life fairytale. I could be Cinderella if I got the prince to kiss me by the end of the ball."

My heart sank.

She said it so I didn't have to: "Not that that happened. Silly for me to think it would, even for a moment." She laughed, but it was one of those slightly hurt laughs, like it still stung, even after all these years.

I wanted to reach out to her again, but considering how she'd rejected my touch last time, I didn't try again. Experience had taught me that while Mama H had infinite comfort to give, she still rarely allowed you to reciprocate. She was an iron pillar, and the fact that she showed me such vulnerability in this moment... it was special. It meant she'd let me in further than she did most people.

"No, I was not chosen that night. Another beautiful, less broken woman without shadows in her eyes was picked."

God, I wanted to hug her. If she would have allowed it, I would have.

"But"—she brightened, looking back at me—"it was what was meant to be." Her eyes were bright. "Because I wasn't chosen, I became what I am today."

What was that, exactly? I wondered.

"I've been able to take care of you girls all these

years. I've been able to take care of the men of the
Order. At first I saw to their"—she rolled her eyes
—"carnal needs. Men are so easy. I worked the
parties that year and eventually just started staying
on and taking on more and more responsibilities
until I ran the household. Eventually they caught
on about who was in charge."

She winked at me, and I laughed out loud.

And then I just blinked. By "working the
parties," she meant... I connected it with my other
limited knowledge of what Rafe had told me over
the years... Orgies. She meant she participated in
the orgies and sex games the Order organized as
part of each Initiation. Mama H and... orgies.

Okay. I blinked. It might take me a minute to
connect these two disparate thoughts and realities.

"So, when your mother was rejected, I showed
her the ropes of how to play the parties, too."

Wait, WHAT?

"*What*?" I screeched, jumping up from the
bench. "Mom worked the sex parties for those old,
saggy-balled bastards? As in like a prostitute?"

"Of course not!" Mama H said, sounding
offended. "Your mother and I were never pros-
titutes."

My mouth gaped open. "Then... why..."

Mama H got to her feet and she had a good two
inches on me. She stared me down. "I'd hoped you

were grown up enough to discuss this, but maybe I was wrong."

She started to walk away. Shit.

"No. No!" I ran to catch up with her and put my hand on her arm. At least she didn't yank away from me. Thank God for small favors.

"No. Mama H, no! I just... This is a lot to process, okay?"

She breathed out, her ruffled feathers calming. She nodded. "All right. Do you want to hear the rest of the story or not?"

Hurriedly, I nodded my head. "Yes. No judgment, I swear. I just want to know what happened to my mother."

Mama H's face clouded over again. She held out her arm to me and I took it. She led us down the little path down closer to the riverbank. "Your mother was never meant for the Oleander lifestyle, not long-term. She enjoyed the Oleander for what it was, but she knew those parties were fantasy. She was always more interested in getting on with her real life. But it was hard to find work. She did what she could, and then on the weekends came and got lost in the most opulent pleasures."

"God, Mama H, enough with the details. This is my mom!"

Mama H tut-tutted. "Your generation is supposed to be all about sexual liberation."

I just squeezed my eyes shut. "Not when it comes to our *parents*."

She laughed. "Anyway. Then you came along, and your mom decided it was time to get serious. I helped her get the job at Rafe's family's house and that was that."

A horrible thought struck me, and I grabbed her arm. "Oh God." I was about to be sick. Pieces started to click into place. "You're saying Mom was having sex at the Oleander. And Rafe's dad was there, and then Mom got pregnant with me—"

But Mama H immediately shook her head vigorously no.

"No, your mother never slept with Rafe's father. *Ever*. I swear to you, as your mother swore to me."

The panic was still alive in my chest though. "How can you be sure?"

Mama H just gave me *the look*. "Your mother's not an idiot. She knew you were interested in Rafe as a teenager. I asked her the same question, but she said it was completely impossible. She never slept with Rafe's father even once. In fact, he was the Initiate who rejected her as his belle. If anything else, his guilt at rejecting her, then someone else knocking her up was part of why he was so eager to give her a job. He'd given some other woman all her dreams and left your mother... well... as she was."

I froze. "So, wait... are you saying one of the other Order members is... my *father*?" I wasn't hesitant about grabbing Mama H this time. I grabbed both of her arms and demanded, "Who? Who is my father?"

"I don't know!" she said. "I swear I don't know which one of them it is!"

I let go of her and stumbled backwards. This couldn't all be real. I was dreaming. No way Mama H had just confessed that she and my mother were rejected belles who'd then spent the next three months fucking various dudes in wild sex parties —oh and during one of those aforementioned gangbangs, some other rich, multi-millionaire fucker had knocked up Mom with *me*.

And then left us. No money. No support. Nothing. Whoever it was had left my mother defenseless; a single mother in an unforgiving world.

Unexpected rage burned through my belly at the realization.

Mom and I had never lived in anything better than a one-bedroom apartment on the bad side of town. Shitty landlords, mice, ants, cockroaches, broken pipes, a toilet that either wouldn't flush or would overflow, no hot water in winter, the list went on and on and on and on—

Meanwhile my baby daddy had lived just miles away in some other mansion, his wife and kids—

holy *shit*—did I have half-siblings?—living in the lap of luxury. Meanwhile Mom fought her entire life to make ends meet.

Another thought struck. "My scholarship to Darlington Prep. Was that real or was that *him*?" Had some anonymous father secretly cared about my education?

Mama H's face dropped to the ground, and she slowly shook her head. "No. No honey, it wasn't your father."

I felt like both raging and crying at the same time. My hands fisted as I fought back emotion. "Why? Why are you telling me all this *now*?" Frankly I might have preferred to go on in ignorance.

Her countenance brightened and that was when she pulled out an envelope, gold letters embossed on it, my name on the invitation. "Because we finally have the chance to fix it. To repair all of the past's mistakes. Rafe is the Initiate. He'll choose you for sure. Finally, you can go through the Trials and get everything that was always denied to your mother. You'll be the one they never saw coming and you can finally claim your birthright."

"But he—" I started but she cut me off.

"It's Rafe. He'll get his head out of this ass long enough to see the amazing woman in front of him when he sees you there. Don't worry, darling. Your time has finally come."

Except she was wrong.

Because Rafe had just rejected me. Again.

And I had just lived up to my mother's legacy all right.

Along with Mama H.

I was another in a long, illustrious line of losers.

Fuck them. Fuck this patriarchal system. Fuck them all!

I took one last look at Rafe with the belle he'd chosen over me and then started to stomp towards the exit.

But right before I could take a single step, the girl in yellow standing in front of Rafe collapsed.

As in, she dropped to the floor like a freakin' stone.

The other women gasped, some screeched. I froze. A couple of men stepped forward, rather calmly considering the situation, and picked her up by her arms.

"Another one down," joked a man from the back of a group of men, and there was snickering laughter.

"Hasn't happened in a few years," another said.

"Is she okay?" Rafe asked, wide-eyed, reaching out a hand uselessly towards the woman who was already being dragged off. She was blinking and looking around even as the Elders pulled her from the room, her silk gown sliding smoothly on the marble floor.

"She just fainted," said one of the Elders, stepping forward. "It happens sometimes. You chose poorly."

Rafe looked around like a deer in a gunsight who realizes he's about to get it. "What does this mean? What happens now?" he gulped hard. "Is it over before I've even started?"

The Elder paused and stared at Rafe critically. The man was familiar, but I couldn't place him. Was he the father of one of Rafe's friends? I'd occasionally run into the families of the powerful through my association with Rafe and his friends, but that didn't mean I'd memorized their faces.

Gah, why was I even still standing here? This was bullshit, and frankly, no longer any of my concern.

I was about to continue my journey out the door and towards a bottle of tequila so I could forget this stupid night had ever happened when suddenly I heard my name.

"You chose poorly, so now we will choose your belle, and you will have one last chance to pass your Initiation. Fallon Perry will be your belle."

I all but choked as I spun around to look at the group gathered on the other side of the ballroom.

Me? How the hell did they even know my name? Why would they choose me? Had Mama H done something? But she couldn't have known Rafe would choose the wimpy blonde in yellow or that—

"Not her," Rafe said, the words spitting out of his mouth like a staccato shotgun blast. "Anyone but her."

They hit their mark. I was shocked I managed to stay on my feet and hated the fucking tears that bit at my eyes. My nose stung and in that moment I fucking *hated* Rafe Jackson. I couldn't believe I'd ever— That I ever thought I'd— That I'd ever felt *anything* for him, that I'd ever—

"It's her or no one and you fail," the Elder said ruthlessly. "It's her or you leave the Oleander tonight in disgrace and never return."

Now Rafe was the one who looked like he'd been blasted by buckshot. His eyes came to me reflecting devastation and confusion.

Another man broke from the pack of men, the fabric of his silver robe swishing smoothly as he crossed the room to me. I could only watch, shocked into silence and stillness by all that was happening. It was only once he got closer that I realized I recognized the man.

It was Rafe's father.

He barely stopped once he got to me. In a swift motion, he reached out and grasped the pearls around my neck. In the same action, he yanked them hard. The silk string broke and pearls scattered across the marble floor, bouncing and dancing away, the tinkling noise the only sound in the otherwise silent room.

Rafe's father took the broken necklace and walked back to his son. When he shoved it towards Rafe, Rafe put out his hand as if reflexively.

"Let's hope you make better decisions from now on, son," his father said, voice hard. "I expect my eldest son to bring me pride and not shame."

"It is done," said the first Elder. "The Initiate's belle has been chosen."

Then the canes began to pound the floor again all over the room.

Holy shit. It looked like I wasn't a reject after all.

I'd just been named a belle of the Order of the Silver Ghost.

5

RAFE

I wanted—

No, I *needed* to speak to her. I needed a moment of privacy so we could discuss what was about to happen. Did she know? Did she know that we were expected to fuck tonight? Right now? Did she know the Elders would be in the room and watching?

How could she?

I only knew because Sully had told me the rumors were true. I was ready for this, or at least as much as I could be. I had prepared for this. But no way could Fallon be ready. She should have chickened out just as the belle in yellow did. She should have run away for her own sake.

If I could just have a moment with her alone, maybe I could talk some sense into her. Maybe if she pulled out of this Trial before we "consummated" the partnership, the Elders would choose another belle and I wouldn't lose the Initiation. Maybe there was still time...

But when we entered the guest room on the second floor, I knew deep down we were too late. This was going to happen whether we liked it or not.

The room was large and had its own fireplace. The king-size, four-post canopy bed barely filled any of the massive space. There was plenty of room for a sitting area with a small couch and two high-back armchairs that sat before the handcrafted mantle. The room had richly-woven rugs, crafted wood furniture, collectible books in a custom-made bookcase, and antiques dating from the civil war era. The large window with thick and luxurious drapes overlooked the pool and rose gardens of the expansive grounds. The Oleander Manor truly was magnificent both inside and out.

I knew, without the Elders even saying so, this would be our home for the next 109 days.

The first beat of the cane announced it was time for the consummation to begin.

Silver cloaks, voyeuristic eyes, and fucked up sexual desires stared upon the empty bed waiting...

Waiting for us to fuck.

And even though I knew he was there... I

refused to look at my father. I couldn't look at him. I couldn't focus on the fact that he was about to watch me fuck my childhood best friend with a room full of spectators.

As if Fallon knew that prolonging the inevitable would only torture us, she unceremoniously removed the light purple dress she wore as she kicked off her heels. She didn't even keep her undergarments on but stripped completely naked without even casting a glance in my direction.

Once nude, she raised her eyes and locked eyes with mine.

Challenge?

Yes, challenge exuded from her tiny frame. She wasn't going to hold up this process. She was ready... ready for me.

Knowing I had to do my part in starting this sick performance, I spun her around to face the bed and pressed my chest up against her back.

I didn't want to see her eyes. I couldn't have Fallon Perry looking at me as I fucked her.

Having the Elders lined up to watch was sick and twisted enough, especially considering one of them was my goddamn father!

But Fallon... I didn't want to look into her soul. I couldn't.

She deserved better than this. She shouldn't be here.

The beating of the canes began, and I knew there was no turning back.

Beat after beat, and I realized they weren't going to stop.

Jesus Christ... we were going to have an eerie soundtrack as we fucked.

I cupped her breasts with each of my hands and pressed my hard cock against the seam of her ass. I shouldn't be hard. I shouldn't be aroused in the slightest, but Fallon was naked, and my cock had a mind of its own.

Brushing my lips against her ear, I whispered, "We don't have to do this. If you tell me to stop, I will."

I didn't want to hear the words, but I would have honored her wishes. It would have meant the end of the Trials, and I didn't want to fail, but at the same time, this wasn't just some belle, some stranger. This woman was too fucking special to allow her to go down this dark rabbit hole by force.

And also, the complete madness in all this was that I *wanted* to fuck her. I wanted my cock buried deep inside of her regardless of our circumstances. What that said about me, I wasn't sure. But my throbbing dick spoke loud and clear. And I wanted to make sure that Fallon actually wanted this too.

I was in the middle of a hellish situation and really should be focusing on getting past the Initiation and make this sex as quick as possible, but her magnetic pull was just too much. When she'd stripped her ball gown off right in front of everyone without an ounce of shame or embarrassment on her face, and briefly looked at me with those sultry eyes laced with challenge, the gloves had come off.

I was a red-blooded man after all, so what did anyone expect? And Fallon was the hottest woman I ever had the pleasure of seeing completely naked.

I brushed my lips on the column of her throat and tried to ignore that Fallon seemed scared, her every muscle tense, her limbs stiff. But holding her softness in my arms, my goal was to make her relax against me, become pliant, languid, because no matter what nightmare we were in the middle of, this was still going to be our first time having sex.

I never thought this day would ever come. And here it was.

"Just do it. Get it over with," she said as she tilted her head more to the side, giving me better access to kiss on her neck, which I didn't dare.

The act of a kiss seemed far too intimate. I couldn't make love to Fallon in front of everyone. *Fuck*, yes... I had no choice. But I sure as hell wasn't going to be loving, sensitive, and romantic while my goddamn father and his old cronies watched on.

Bending her over so her palms rested on the mattress, I readied myself for what would come next. Massaging her breasts between my fingers, my cock throbbed even harder when Fallon quietly mewled in pleasure. Her tiny whimper of lust had my cock twitching against my pants, begging to be satiated.

"Do it," she purred while reaching behind her, grabbing hold of my thigh with one hand and pulling me even closer to her perfectly-shaped ass.

Lowering my hand away from teasing one of her nipples, I ran my fingertips down her firm belly to her mound, cupping it while I nearly growled into her ear. Finding her clit, I pressed lightly and moved my finger in a gentle and circular motion.

I loved hearing the catch in her breath and thrived on how it was obvious she enjoyed my touch and even wanted more when she gyrated against my hand. I knew I could make her cum this way if I wanted to take more time and all eyes weren't on us—maybe I would save that for another day.

Unzipping my pants and taking hold of my cock with my other hand, I guided my dick past the folds of her pussy and eased inside her silky warmth with enough pause for her to adjust to my girth.

Blocking out my surroundings, I began pushing

and pulling, feeling the walls of her sex squeeze tightly around me as I did so.

I was inside her. I was fucking Fallon... and it felt so right. So fucking right.

Fallon clung to my hand that still rested on her pussy, moaning softly. "Rafe," she said barely louder than a whisper between her gasps.

The sound of pleasure leaving her lips captivated me completely—impressive considering we weren't alone.

The passion built with every movement, and I felt an impending orgasm build. Part of me wanted to be done, end the night, but a more powerful and controlling part of me wanted to make this feeling last a little longer.

I wanted to claim her harder and with more force. Fallon was finally mine, and after tonight, there would be no question. We couldn't turn back time after this. We couldn't just go back to being friends. My cock was buried deep inside of her, and as I pressed my balls against the firmness of her ass, I knew we had crossed a line to possession.

She was mine. Truly *My Fallon* now.

It was animalistic in belief. Primal. But I couldn't fight the carnal urge to fuck her longer than planned. I didn't want to leave the tight warmth of her pussy.

As if we were connected by mind and not just

body, Fallon pushed her ass hard against me, driving me deeper inside. Her simple action silently told me she didn't want gentle and loving, but rather wanted a true fucking just as much as I did.

She gave a sharp gasp as I thrust into her with the full force that I had been holding back. Wrapping her dark hair in my fist, I gave it a tug until she turned to look back at me.

Her eyes were glazed, her mouth slightly open as she nodded her understanding, and I could actually feel the walls of her pussy constrict around my cock. It was all I needed to truly start fucking her with fury.

I moved my finger, which still rested on her clit, determined to make her cum right alongside of me.

I wasn't going to last much longer but waited until I could hear her repeated moans of absolute desire become cries of completion. The spasms of the velvet walls of her pussy around my cock were all it took for me to explode inside her.

Electric jolts of pleasure ran through every vein in my body. Never in my entire life had I experienced something so erotic, so tantalizing, and so fucking unbelievable as fucking Fallon Perry.

I wanted to fuck her again.

And again.

I only wanted to fuck Fallon Perry forever and ever… consumed.

It took Fallon pulling away to convince me that I hadn't just died or had an out-of-body experience. Every ounce of skin on my body buzzed in euphoria. This woman had captivated not only my body, but my entire being.

Feeling her shudder, however, reality sunk in. I realized that I could feel goose bumps on her skin as I caressed her back.

She was naked. Vulnerable to the eyes of the Elders—

The canes began to bang hard against the floor, and what had been a moment of pure bliss had suddenly returned to hell with silver-cloaked devils all around me.

With the final beats of the canes, the Elders left the room.

Now, the true test would begin.

We were alone to face our demons together.

Without saying a single word, I lowered the bedding and then guided her to bed for sleep.

There was so much I wanted to say. So much I wanted to discuss. We needed to come up with a plan. We needed to talk about the fact that we had just had sex and what did that mean. Hell, we needed to catch up after years of being apart.

But not tonight.

We'd had enough for one night.

As if I were doing nothing more than tucking in a lover for bed, I covered her up and watched her close her eyes.

Yes, we needed to close our eyes and maybe...

Just maybe...

When we opened them again, this would all be over.

But when I stripped and crawled into bed beside her, I couldn't resist. I had to. I had to move a piece of her raven hair lying across her face and tuck it behind her ear just as I had always done when we were young.

Her eyes opened.

And we both just stared.

6

FALLON

When I woke up, it was to find his eyes on me. Our eyes caught, just as they had last night, after he'd— After we'd—

My heartbeat had still been pulsing so hard, his cum spilling out of me. Even now, the morning after, the memory of his body inside mine after all these years... Just the memory was so visceral it was like it was still happening.

The shudder started again in my body, and I jerked out of bed, horrified.

"Fallon, can we—" he started to say, but I fled to the bathroom and slammed the door behind me before I could hear the rest of that sentence.

No. No we could not.

I slammed my hands over my face, then dragged them down. Holy shit. Ho_ly *shit*. I'd finally had sex with Rafe Jackson. And it had been, oh God, it had been—

I glimpsed the hollow woman in the mirror across the vanity.

She looked shell-shocked.

Because sex with Rafe had been earth-shattering. I mean, I'd always suspected it would be. But to finally have it confirmed, at the worst possible moment—

I squeezed my eyes shut, but that didn't help anything, because I just remembered every touch, every caress of his body against mine. The way he pushed my hair behind my ear afterwards, the way he always used to when we were kids, the past and the present blurring and making my heart burst open with hope and agony.

My eyes snapped open at the thought. *No.* Dear God, *no.* How many times could a girl put her heart through the blender over one boy?

That wasn't what I was here for.

I was here to get what was owed me.

I gave one decisive nod and then stomped over to the shower, turning it to the hottest setting I could. I would wash that boy off my skin and out of my system once and for all.

Half an hour later, we were seated at a ridiculously long, elegant table, me at one end, Rafe about twelve feet away at the other end. This seating arrangement suited me just fine. Much easier to ignore him if he wasn't right in my face.

I hadn't given him much of a chance to say anything to me after I'd gotten out of the shower and dressed, even though he'd tried. But I'd spent most of the last half hour in the shower, then flounced out just in time for breakfast.

I could tell he was steaming and had plenty to say to me, in that Rafe way of his. He had a terrible poker face. There was obviously something he wanted to get off his chest, maybe *many* somethings, but frankly, I wasn't in the mood.

The shower had helped my resolve. I was here to do a job and not Rafe Jackson or anybody else was going to keep me down anymore. I was a woman with a plan.

"This is ridiculous." Rafe finally tossed down his silverware with a loud clank, which I could only just hear from so far away. "We need to talk, Fallon, and I refuse to sit here and shout across the breakfast table."

I just kept eating my omelet. Whatever he would or would not refuse to do was frankly none of my problem.

"Fallon. Fallon, can you even hear me?" he said louder.

I continued ignoring him. The cook here was *excellent.* When Mama H came to collect our dishes, I'd have to tell her to compliment the cook. The omelet was mouthwatering, with some kind of fancy white cheese in the middle. A far cry from the Kraft singles I'd toss in mine growing up while Mom worked a double shift because Rafe's family threw some party and they needed her to clean up after them.

One time when she described the fancy party they'd had and all the fancy food, I asked her if she could bring home leftovers next time. Her face had clouded over, and she'd hurriedly explained Mrs. Jackson preferred to throw out the leftovers than allow the "help" to take any home. Mrs. Jackson thought it would disincentivize them to serve as well, or maybe they'd hold some back, if they knew they could take home what wasn't eaten.

I stabbed the next bite of omelet a little harder than was necessary.

"Enough, Fallon," Rafe said, standing up, leaving his breakfast behind and walking down towards my end of the table. He towered above me, looking down.

"Are we gonna talk about last night?" he demanded. Oh, he'd really worked himself up.

Good to know some things never change. Rafe could never hold it in long when he was upset about something. It would blow one way or another, and in his repressed fucking family, usually that meant with me, playing rough when we were kids and then later, driving fast cars, staying out late with me, the town goth girl everyone else rejected.

For a long time, I thought that's all I was—hanging out with me was one big Fuck You to his parents, his one lingering rebellion. Or rather, like everything else, a desperate cry for attention from his uptight family. Especially his mom, who completely ignored him in favor of his so-called golden-boy brother Timothy who Hung The Moon in her eyes.

But then Timothy died. And mommy dearest finally turned her eyes on forgotten little Rafe.

So naturally, he had no more use for me. In reality, I'd always been as disposable as those party leftovers. He'd been using me just like his family used my mother. But at least they'd paid her.

What did I get out of it? A broken heart and a ticket out of town on the first bus, courtesy of his mother who felt her New Golden Child didn't need any more distractions. At least not ones as uncouth as the undesirable bastard daughter of the help who looked like the rejected offspring of Marilyn

Manson and Ozzy Osbourne. I'm sure Rafe got a whole new fleet of fast cars to drive. Mommy Jackson did so love to spoil her favorites.

He certainly didn't use any of them to come after me, even though I sent him repeated emails in my weaker moments, praying I'd misunderstood things, that it had just been grief for his lost brother that had kept him silent, longing for even a couple of words from him even if they were: "not now" or "I need time".

But those never came.

Only silence.

"Why the hell are you here?" Rafe continued. There was fire in his eyes. He was furious at me.

I wanted to laugh. After all this time, after we'd had *sex* for the first time, these were the first words out of his mouth?

"Are you crazy?" he blasted me, so upset his handsome face was getting those red blotches high on his cheekbones I'd always found so irresistibly sexy when we were teenagers. "Do you even know what you're getting yourself into? You have no idea!"

But then I fought through the haze of his sexiness and how the closeness of his body heat was *doing things* to me to focus on his words.

Mistake. Or maybe my saving grace.

Because every word out of his mouth only

pissed me off more. "I'm crazy? *I'm* crazy?" My voice went up about an octave. I shoved my chair back and stood up so that he could no longer tower over me, looking down his stupid gorgeous nose at me.

I glared at him. "I know this might be incomprehensible to your little pea brain, but I am a full-grown woman who knows her own mind. Yes, I know what I'm here for. Yes, I know what I'm getting into." I briefly glanced around the room, the sturdy, aged and stained floorboards and wallpaper, and thought of how my own mother might have once walked through this very same room.

My eyes flashed back to Rafe. "Your family kept me down my whole fucking life. I'm not going to let any Jackson tell me what I can or cannot do ever again."

Rafe's brow crumpled, like he was confused. "What are you even talking about?"

God, boys could be so obtuse. If he couldn't connect the dots, I wasn't going to spell it out for him.

I put a finger in his face. "I'm here to get what's owed to me. What I *deserve*. What my *family* deserves. And you are not going to stop me."

Rafe just shook his head. "You don't know what you're saying. You don't know what this place is—"

I scoffed at that. This place had used up and

spit my mom out as an impoverished single mother with zero support. And Rafe thought *I* didn't know what this place was? I was pretty sure *he* was the one who needed an education on the Oleander's history and what really went on here.

But no, that would require him actually *listening* and maybe, just maybe, being willing to admit he wasn't a master of the universe who knew everything. Something I was pretty sure no one in his family had ever, *ever* done. So, I wasn't holding my breath. Rafe had proven to me long ago that he was a Jackson through and through.

Rafe's brows drew together. Oh, I was really frustrating him now. That was the face he got when he wasn't getting his way and he didn't like it. This was almost fun.

"Fallon, stop it, this isn't funny. This isn't like stealing a candy bar from the corner store when we were kids. I'm not joking. This is serious. You shouldn't be here."

You shouldn't be here. Dagger to the heart. Because, oh right, he'd rather have fucked some other woman last night. The delicate little fainting blonde.

Fuck him. Fuck Rafe Jackson, that he still had any ability to hurt me. I felt my eyebrows rise to my hairline. I got right in his face.

"No, Rafe, you're right. You thinking you can tell me what to do certainly isn't funny. At all."

He huffed out a breath through his nose like an angry bull, the spots on his cheeks getting even brighter. "You aren't even trying to listen to me. I'm trying to *protect* you—"

At my loud scoff the spots in his cheeks turned even redder, though I seriously wouldn't have thought that was possible at this point. He was going to light on fire any second at this rate. Still, I couldn't resist poking the bear.

"God save me from the 'protection' of anyone with the last name Jackson. I've seen how your kind *protect*—you only protect your own, even when to the world it looks like charity. I know the truth."

Like giving the poor little housekeeper's daughter a "scholarship" to prep school because Rafe's father felt guilty about not choosing her mother during the Initiation. Instead, he doomed her to a life of just above poverty, all for the privilege of cleaning up after him and his wife for the rest of Mom's life. The least he could do was provide her daughter—a bastard daughter fathered by some known or unknown friend of his—with an education.

Either that or Rafe's mom was terrified my mom would spill her guts about Rafe's dad and what went on in the Oleander. Mama H theorized that if Mrs. Jackson would have had her way, Mrs. Jackson would have run us out on a rail the second she found out about any of it. But Rafe's dad put his foot down, and she'd come up with the idea of paying for my school as a means of leverage and silencing Mom instead.

Until Timothy died. Then Mr. Jackson stopped giving a shit about everything, apparently. And Mrs. Jackson got rid of me like she'd always wanted.

Rafe stepped back from me, looking baffled. "What are you *talking* about?"

Now I really did want to laugh. He hadn't known? It had tormented me, wondering if he'd been in on it, if they'd ever told him—if he knew his "best friend's" education was being paid for by his own parents as an insidious form of manipulation. After all, who could fault them for such a generous act? If anyone knew of it, they'd think I should shut my mouth and be *grateful*.

Certainly not my mother, who was desperate for me to have a better life than she did. She wanted bigger things for her daughter than the business end of a mop and dustpan.

Look how far I've come, Mama, I thought sardonically. *Right back to where you began. But I'm gonna get it right this time. I'm going to get everything they owed you.*

"How was breakfast?" Mama H's cheery voice broke into our tense standoff. "Did you like the omel—" She broke off mid-word when she saw how we were posed, in each other's faces, obviously both frayed and upset.

She let out a long breath, then set down the little box with a black bow she'd carried in with her. She put her hands on her hips and whistled, so loud it felt like it pierced my eardrums. I winced and covered my ears. She waved at me to put them down.

"Enough of this. Whatever lover's squabble you two are having can wait."

She didn't wait for me to object that she had absolutely *not* walked into a lover's quarrel, but she was already barreling ahead.

"Enough of this, the both of you," she chastised us like we were still small children. "You"—she pointed at Rafe—"take a seat." Then she pointed her sharp finger at me. "You, too. Sit."

I obeyed. When Mama H got *that* voice, you sat down and shut up. I had common sense, and apparently so did Rafe, because he did the same as me. We'd both felt the wrath of Mrs. H many, many times as children.

"Yes, ma'am," Rafe said. I'd managed not to say

yes ma'am along with him, but only by biting my bottom lip. My hands were still tucked obediently in my lap. I didn't call Mama H *Mama* for no reason. She could put the fear of God into any soul when she got that tone.

"Now you listen to me, do you hear me? You two are going to need each other, and I won't see any more of this pettiness. Rafe"—she arched a glaring eyebrow at him, but even though it wasn't directed at me, I cowered in my seat—"you may not have wanted it to be Fallon going through these Trials with you, and I understand you want to protect her. You want to protect everybody. But you're going to have to grow up someday and realize that a woman like Fallon can take care of herself."

Ha. I looked over at Rafe and just barely kept myself from sticking out my tongue. Take *that* Rafe Jackson. Even Mama H saw my side of it.

"Now, don't you go thinking you're so high and mighty, lassie," Mama H said next, zeroing her laser glare my direction.

I sat back, shoulders straight, feeling skewered like a bug underneath a magnifying glass. Oh shit, why did I have a feeling it was my turn now?

"Yes, I know being here isn't all hearts and flowers, but it never was going to be, and you were deluding yourself if you thought any different. I tried to prepare you, but you can't really know how the Trials will test you until you step under this roof and feel the pressure of these walls. They carry secrets and dreams you can't even fathom."

She waved her curved pointer finger at the both of us. "The only way the two of you have a *hope* of surviving—much less thriving in these Trials that will test your mettle, your will, your very *soul*—is if you work together and lean on one another. And then you have a chance, and I do mean just a *chance* of passing these Trials. You never know what they're going to throw at you next. Not even I know what's coming, but I do know that the only couples who make it are the ones who let go of their egos and cling to each other for strength."

Rafe's head bobbed up and down. "Yes, ma'am. We'll do better." He looked over at me, his eyebrows knit in sincerity as he reached out and took my hand. "I'll do better. I'm sorry, Fallon. I swear I'll do better."

Well, what the fuck was I supposed to do with him being all sweet like that? I still wanted to be pissed at him. That was much easier to understand and compartmentalize.

A sweet, sensitive Rafe was just a mind-fuck.

But I wasn't fool enough not to heed Mama H's warning and advice. So, reluctantly, I squeezed Rafe's hand back.

It didn't mean anything. So, I'd work *with* him instead of against him. We had common goals, that was all. It wasn't like I agreed to marry the man. Just to work with him since he was the only partner I had.

I was strictly being practical.

A flash of Rafe's naked body thrusting into mine from last night played out on sudden repeat in my head.

Ha, practical. Yeah, that was it. My wanting to work with him instead of against him had absolutely *nothing* to do with the fact that it likely meant getting my body underneath his again and feeling him inside me. Again and again and again if what I'd heard about these Trials was true in even the smallest measure.

So, I squeezed Rafe's hand and arched an eyebrow of my own. "I'm in if you are."

Rafe took a deep breath, his large chest expanding outwards. But then he let it out in a huge whoosh of air and nodded. "Fine. I'm in, too. You, Fallon Perry, are my belle."

And then, more under his breath as Mama H beamed at us, I didn't miss his following murmur: "God have mercy on us both."

"Oh death, oh death, oh death," an Elder chanted as we all filed outside the Oleander Manor to the large wraparound porch.

Candles were lit, adding to the fiery light put out by the hanging gas lanterns. Glass bottles of various colors dangled from the awning, and I wouldn't be a true Southern boy if I didn't know that their purpose was to chase away the spirits of the night. Fireflies flickered in the thick and sticky air of the night. An owl hooted in the distance as if warning me to run as fast as I could away from what would occur this night.

Elders in their silver cloaks lined up near the large entryway and the members flanked behind us. Both Fallon and I awaited what would come next with bated breath.

The Elder continued on with his chant. "We ask you dubious haints to leave the Oleander. Cross over to the other side and not enter our dwellings."

I watched the Elders raise their palms to the covered porch they stood beneath and point to the arched architecture.

"We paint our entrance blue to chase the haints away. But tonight, since we are sure there is one particular ghost haunting us now, we offer the belle to be covered in haint blue. This is our offering to you." The Elder spoke as if we were surrounded by our deceased ancestors and they were all listening.

Chills ran through me as I reached for Fallon's hand, only to have her pull away from it.

I noticed the cans of paint surrounding the Elders and tried to figure out exactly what was about to occur. The entryway was already painted haint blue and had been for centuries as was tradition. So why the paint? And why so much?

"Fallon Perry. You are to stand beneath the blue to help us chase away the spirit of Rafe's older brother. He's here. His haint is here taunting us, and it's our job to chase him away. We'll paint your body blue with our hands. Every. Single. Inch. The hands of the man will join as one."

The words were like a punch to the gut. Rage

surged through me. My brother? They were not allowed to talk about my brother! How dare they? How fucking dare—

My fury came to a screeching halt when Fallon began to move forward.

"Absolutely not," I said under my breath, grabbing her by the arm and tugging her back toward me harshly.

Fallon's breath hitched, but she yanked her arm away from my grip and took a step away from me. "I got this. Don't you dare fuck this up."

"You're not a whore," I hissed. "You shouldn't let them touch you. You aren't a goddamn whore."

Her head snapped in my direction and daggers shot from her eyes. "Exactly!"

She moved toward the entryway by the front door and stood with her chin held high and shoulders back. She stood naked with the light from the gas lanterns reflecting off her flawless skin.

I closed my eyes briefly wondering if I could just block out all that was about to occur. I didn't want to watch this. I couldn't. No way could I just stand back and let these wrinkled dicks touch her.

But when I opened my eyes, I saw her staring at me. Silently telling me to remain where I was.

"Let the Trial begin," an Elder declared, hitting his cane hard on the planked porch. "Chase the haints away!"

Cans of paint were lined up on the porch beckoning, and several members of the Order dipped their hand into the blue, approached Fallon as if she were a blank canvas, and began painting her with their caresses. Hands groped her, hands invaded, hands touched and stained her skin with their sins. Blue-covered hands slapped her bare ass, leaving behind blue handprints. Some stroked her pussy; others rubbed her breasts as if she were nothing but a statue.

Fallon remained in place, emotionless, blank.

Her glare was locked with mine, and her defiance challenged my rage.

How could she?

Why would she?

And why would I just stand here and watch as these men violated her body with their touch?

I moved forward to put a stop to it, and Fallon shouted, "Stay!"

I froze, but the Elders and the members all continued on as I watched. Her body dripped in paint, her hair wet with the color, and yet she appeared pale as man after man marked her as nothing but a broken belle.

I looked to Montgomery for help, but he simply stood with his clean hands at his sides. His eyes were focused toward a weeping willow tree in the distance near the cemetery. It was as if he could actually see the spirits of our forefathers watching on. Montgomery was here physically, but his mind had detached. I suppose I needed to learn this if I were going to be able to pass the Initiation myself.

Block the evil out.

Chase the haints away...

"Rafe Jackson," one of the Elders spoke, breaking me from the flurry of blue hell that I was cast in. "It is your job to chase away Timothy Jackson. This is your Trial tonight. You must."

And how the fuck did they expect me to do that?

By standing here watching my old best friend get violated by every rich fuck in the South?

My Fallon, I thought with a possessiveness that caught me off guard.

Only mine.

But she wouldn't let me help her.

Used goods. That's the only way the Elders saw this belle before us. She was covered in blue paint. Fresh handprints covered the older, drying ones. They just kept going. Touching. Leaving behind those invasive markings of what they claimed as theirs.

Fallon stood stoically and took each touch with her prideful stare locked with mine.

But finally...

She had enough. Her eyes told me. Her

slumped shoulders announced it. Now she needed me.

It was about goddamn time.

I stepped forward, and she nodded.

That was all I needed to clear the distance between us. I took her by her blue-covered arm and pulled her to me, away from the last two men still touching her. I hadn't forgiven her for her defiant act, but no way would I let another man touch her again tonight.

I too had had enough.

The Elders began pounding their canes as one said, "Claim the belle. Chase the haints away by claiming the belle beneath the blue."

Standing stiffly, surrounded by softness, my body stirred at the brush of warm lips against the side of my neck. "Make this all go away," she whispered.

The gentle caress sent shivers coursing down my spine, branching off deliciously at my chest and gut then shooting with a jolt of sensation to my already-hard cock.

Fallon grinded against me, her smooth legs rubbing against my pants, forever staining them in blue. Her nipples pressed against my chest, as her eyes looked up at me in silent plea.

She couldn't take the assault anymore. She couldn't stand their touch, their trespass of the woman she once was, their claiming of what didn't belong to them.

When my cock twitched in response to her need, nudging against her thigh, her mouth curved into a seductive smile, and she gave a low, throaty mewl, the heated exhale washing over my skin.

"Touch me. I only want *you* to touch me," she finally confessed in her sultry voice.

"I thought you had this handled." I grinned.

What fool wouldn't step in and do exactly as she asked? But part of me wanted her to pay some more. Or at the very least beg me to help.

She'd forced me to stand there and watch these assholes do to her as they wished, and she all but forbade me from stepping in. Her stubborn pride nearly drove me mad, and *now* she wanted me?

I should make her pay. I should—

Fingers slid along my stomach, gliding over the hard plane that rippled in reaction. She inched downward, past my tense lower abdominal muscles, and beyond jutting hip bones to where I longed for her touch the most.

Not making me wait long, she unfastened my pants, lowered them as fast as she could, and encircled my dick, squeezing in a tight fist before parting her plump, paint-splattered lips.

Blocking out all that was around me the best I could, I took hold of her shoulders, feeling the wetness of the paint coat my fingers and pushed her down to her knees before me.

I didn't want her hand. I wanted her goddamn mouth.

Her tongue slipped out and licked the tip. Her husky moan of delight while lapping at the end of my cock proved she was willing to pay her penance.

She was mine, and she better damn well know it. And it was time that every member of the Order witnessed it for themselves. Those fuckers could touch all they wanted, but at the end of this, I would get to have so much more. Only me.

Her lashes fluttered open, and she gazed up at me, eyes dark and sparkling with desire as a grin tilted up the corners of her luscious pink mouth. Paint-soaked hair clung to her face, her shoulders, and dripped down her back.

My body spurred me to act, to end the unnecessary torture of her light tease. I wanted her to swallow me deep and make me cum as all the spectators watched on with envy.

When she enveloped the head, her incredible heat, and the slow circling of the tip with her tongue became pure torment. The inability to control the urge to order her to open wider and suck harder proved I had little patience left.

Gruffly, I took hold of her hair with both my

hands, squeezing excess blue from the strands, and demanded, "Fuck me with your mouth."

Not hesitant in the least, she eagerly swallowed at least half my length on the next glide while I closed my eyes, reveling in the wicked suction and the warm wet haven she created.

"Deeper," I commanded with a husky growl, guiding her by fistfuls of hair. "Let me fuck that face of yours."

My animalistic need to mark her as mine overpowered the sick and twisted setting I was thrust in. On the porch of the Oleander Manor, surrounded in haint paint... I had my dick sucked by my old childhood friend.

What could be more fucked up than that?

A sigh of pleasure escaped my lips when she slid my cock along her tongue, almost to the back of her throat. To take all of me without gagging required practice, something I would happily offer to assist her with in the future.

Still needing more, I sank my fingers deeper into her thick hair and set the pace. Not so quick to bring me to completion, but with enough speed and friction to keep me on the edge.

I watched through eyes half-lidded from my rising passion as she bobbed up and down steadily, with little guidance. I'd drive harder when ready for more. For the moment, I wanted to savor and revel in her skills at giving oral pleasure.

Her rigorous work accelerated my heart rate, gradually building my need into what was shaping up to be the most explosive climax of my life. Adding to my pleasure, a soft hand swept down to my balls, caressing with her fingertips. The play upped my response as she cupped my aching balls and massaged. Her hand moved in tandem while she continued to suck, her tongue licking and circling the sensitive tip, until my back arched reflexively.

Near the end of my tolerance, my hands curled around her head as my hips thrust upward, driving me even deeper. I fucked her mouth the same way I took her pussy last night—thoroughly claiming every inch.

She didn't resist, opening wider in eager acceptance. Her own sweet moans of pleasure filled the air, joining my gruff, primal groans.

"Touch yourself," I ordered, watching her spread her legs and obeying like the naughty and yet very good girl she was.

I knew the Elders would appreciate this sign of dominance and submission, but that wasn't the only reason for my request.

I wanted her to cum. I wanted her to end this night in pleasure rather than nightmare. Even for a split moment, I wanted her to escape this den of vipers.

Looking down, I watched her splayed fingers slide over her belly and mound and disappear between her thighs. I could imagine the intense heat of her pussy, the wetness increasing while she avidly worked her clit. Which only made me want to explode more with the thought.

Thrusting faster, while sliding my cock over her greedy, slurping tongue, I careened headlong toward a shattering climax. "Fuck your pussy and get ready to cum with me."

Her muffled agreement vibrated around my cock and her body writhed, matching the rhythm of my own as I pumped into her mouth. Low and rumbling, I groaned my pleasure. Both hands held her head as I drove into her mouth, taking all she willingly gave.

The next moment, while her mewls of release rang in my ears, my body tensed, sending my seed pulsing down her throat.

While tremors rocked me from the root of my core, I roared with a need to be fucking her. I needed her pussy, and I needed it now. Fallon had only whetted my appetite for more.

The Elders wanted a show.

The Elders wanted to chase the hauntings away.

What better way than to fill this haint-blue entryway with glass bottles swinging around us? With the voyeuristic lust of all the men standing around in their silver cloaks, I would give them exactly what they wanted as a good recruit would do.

Fallon waited on her knees, looking up at me with puffy lips. I released her hair and placed my hands on both sides of her face as I lowered myself on top of her. I wanted to blanket her body with mine. With my mass over hers, the Elders would only see the rise and fall of my ass as I fucked her. She would be my secret. What I tasted, what I touched, what I smelled and got to engulf myself in, would only be mine.

Mine.

And I stared at her. I stared at her as if I could eat her whole.

Fallon was mine, all mine; I would never share her with anyone.

How beautiful she was in paint the color of water as if she were a siren emerging from the sea. To feel her against my inner thigh hot and ready, my own desire wholly evident with my hard cock ready for more, even as my body still recovered from the mind-blowing blowjob.

She reached out to touch my face, then pressed her hand to my chest, feeling the heavy thuds of my heart. She sighed and closed her eyes.

Never had I imagined her skin would be so warm and smooth to my touch or that her dark hair flowing all around her would feel so silky. I had fantasized about Fallon before in my past... but never... never could I have imagined just how fucking amazing she was.

The canes began to beat against the weathered wood of the porch in demand for more. The Elders were tired of waiting. They wanted action just as much as my cock wanted it.

We had fucked for them before, and no doubt tonight wouldn't be the last. But for me... it was different. The primal need to mark her as mine had consumed my every thought and action since the first hand of paint touched her body.

Canes continued on.

I couldn't just lie on top of her, shielding her naked body from their eyes for long.

Taking action, I traveled my fingers down to her pussy and heard her sharp intake of breath. Still gazing at her, I thrust my finger inside to make sure she was wet and ready. Never removing my devouring gaze from her, I took in every inch of her face to make sure she wasn't too embarrassed that we had a full audience as I was about to fuck her... again.

But she was far too gone in the same lust and need as me to feel any embarrassment. I could feel it without a single word spoken. Her only moment of shyness came when I removed my finger and ran her own essence on the plumpness of her lower lip.

"I'm going to fuck you," I whispered, though I think the fact was quite obvious.

Her shyness flew away as she nodded and licked her lips.

Fresh heat inflamed my body, desire curling inside me. Everything was heightened, all my senses were converging together. Fallon moaned and arched her back as I placed my mouth on her breast, licking the limited amount of flesh not marred with blue paint. My mouth and hands were everywhere, kissing, biting, stroking every inch that had not been touched by another.

Her gasps and writhing told me I was bringing her desire to a boil that was on the cusp of spilling over with every touch, scorched with every kiss burned, and soon she'd beg for more. She'd scream out my name in need.

Yes, the Elders would hear her call my name.

Not Timothy's.

The second son.

She would demand the second son to fuck her.

It wouldn't be haint-blue paint chasing away

the spirit of my dead brother. It would be the cries of the belle beneath me.

This Trial was mine. This belle was mine.

When my lips found the crook of her neck, she parted her thighs wider in invitation.

With the tip of my dick still poised at the entrance of her tight little hole, I stared intently into her eyes. "It's just you and me. Just us," I whispered. "Ignore them. Ignore."

She wrapped her arms around me, then cried into my shoulder as I pushed inside her so slowly and with such care that it seemed time had stood still. There was only pleasure, deep radiating pleasure as our bodies merged as one. She put her lips to my neck as I drove deeper and deeper into her. The world became a distant blur shrinking down to just us in this intense and erotic moment. The secret torch I had carried for her for so long, *so long* had been lit into a furnace and all I could do was let the heat from it burn as it reached its peak.

And then finally... Fallon howled out my name, over and over.

My name. Mine.

Pleasure rippled through me, and long waves erupted from inside as I growled my own climax.

She wrapped her legs even tighter around me, holding me inside her as we both allowed our bodies to recover. I wanted to savor every last bit of this incredible moment before our reality would sink back in.

She held me tightly. She dragged her hands up the length of my back and up to my head, threading her fingers through my hair. I could feel her heartbeat hammering in time to mine, thrilled to know that she too had felt the intensity I had experienced.

With the sound of canes hitting the wooden planks of the porch, I knew the Elders were satisfied.

Bang after bang as the nightmare returned. The tidal wave of evil came crashing down on our satiated bodies.

The canes reverberated off the wood, pound after pound.

Trial complete.

Not wanting to stand there under watchful eyes any longer, I violently put my cock away, lifted Fallon's painted body into my arms, and stormed toward the lake to wash this paint off, leaving the ghosts of the Oleander trapped in the haint-blue entrance.

"Did we pass the Trial?" Fallon asked as she nuzzled her face against me.

8

FALLON

"Yeah." His voice was thick as he answered. "I think we passed."

I slumped against his chest. "Thank God." He carried me in the darkness. I wasn't sure where we were going, but I also didn't care.

We'd done it again.

I'd felt him inside me, and it turned out the first time wasn't just a fluke. I'd never felt anything like — Sex wasn't usually— I mean, yes, Jeoffrey and I had slept together, but not very often, and I'd never really found anything that special about it. It was almost a duty to perform, something a good girl-friend did.

But with Rafe, it was...

It made me suspect that Jeoffrey and I had never been doing it the right way. That there was always some missing component, a physical act devoid of... well, connection or intimacy.

All Rafe had to do, though, was touch any part of his skin to mine.

Then my body lit up in ways I didn't even know were possible.

My body flushed with the orgasm he'd given me while deep inside me—another thing I had thought was a myth, along with intimacy during sex. The magazines said that penetrative sex could make women orgasm, but I'd just thought that was more of a fantasy than reality for most women, or that there was something wrong with me and I just didn't work that way.

Um. Well, apparently there was a man who could make me come like that.

And, of course, it had to be Rafe. Because God had a sick sense of humor.

Still, I couldn't stop clutching at his neck. If I only had a few more moments of holding him so close, of feeling his chest pressed against my body as he held me while he carried me—

I sighed, all the fight having been fucked out of me, and slumped against him. For once in my life, I stopped fighting and gave in.

But then it was always so easy to give in to Rafe. It always had been. He was the one person I ever let slip underneath my concrete walls, and it looked like he still knew the way in, even after all these years.

I was sure I'd be annoyed as fuck about it in the morning, but for right now? I let out another satisfied breath, releasing all the fear and anger and distress from having all those others touch me.

Finally, it was just me and Rafe.

Me, Rafe, a starlit sky, and soon I heard the lapping sound of the water against the shore. We'd made it to the lake.

I pressed my ear against Rafe's chest, wanting to hear his heartbeat. Wanting to feel the life pulsing within him before he put me down. Before I lost his warmth.

I'd made his tux filthy, but he didn't seem to care. He hadn't even hesitated in picking me up. A rush of feelings hit me all at once. Conflicting emotions. Some faraway part deep inside me shouting that this wasn't safe. That I was only opening myself up to him hurting me again.

But listening to that voice meant pulling away from him, and I just couldn't do it yet. Not yet. Just a little longer. A little longer and then I'd remember everything else. All my reasons. My reasons had seemed so important earlier. Reasons to stay away from him. Reasons to always protect myself. To shield myself like a soldier going into battle. Shields up, always, then no one could ever hurt me; they'd never get close enough to stab at my fleshy bits. When they left me, I wouldn't feel like a gaping abyss had opened up inside my chest that could never be filled by anyone else.

I'd been so devastated when I'd gotten to the boarding school Mrs. Jackson had paid for me to be sent to in the middle of our senior year. I'd only had a few months left, but she couldn't allow that. No, I was too dangerous. I was a disaster she had to prevent.

But after I'd disappeared from Rafe's world, my life had gone on.

Did he even ever wonder about me? Did he think about what my life was like, those endless days filled without him?

The new school had been horrible.

Wretched.

I thought California was supposed to be filled with nice, chilled-out surfers and hippie-type people.

Well, maybe their parents had been hippies and taught at Berkeley, but that didn't stop their children from being nightmares.

They were not glad to have a weird goth girl show up in their class at the very end of their high school experience. I was a very unwelcome addition. They did not hesitate in letting me know their feelings on the subject.

I thought some of the petty bullshit they pulled was only the kind of thing you saw on TV. Some of the boys actually dunked one of the other scholarship kids in the trash can. Like, completely upside down in the trash can, his scrawny leg sticking out. Then they'd knocked the trashcan over.

They hadn't bothered with me too much until I ran over and helped him out. The boy didn't thank me. He just scurried away and then their wrath turned to me.

I spent the rest of the three months with *Trailer Trash Slut* painted on the inside of my locker, because they wanted to show they had all the power. Even the power to access my things. I finally stopped leaving things in my locker and just hefted around all my books with me all day long. My back hurt by the end of each day, but at least they couldn't fuck with my things.

Not engaging with them didn't make it better, though. They just found new ways to torture me. One girl especially, Becca, really hated me. Her father was the president of the school's Board of Governors, their fancy name for a School Board. She could get away with murder at that school and no one would ever say a thing.

She emptied about twenty pudding cups into my locker and when it all started to smell and drip out, I was the one who got in trouble for it. There were constant comments about my hygiene, as if just because I was poor, I must not know how to shower regularly even though I was always hyper conscious of it.

The boys would touch me in the hallway as they passed me, sometimes approaching in a giant group I couldn't escape. One of them was Becca's boyfriend.

So, I got further punished by her for her boyfriend's casual daily assaults.

Part of me was just like, seriously? Who even had such time for such petty bullshit? Becca Whitley did. She fucking delighted in it.

"So..." Rafe finally broke into the silence, setting me on my feet. Instantly, I hated the cold. It was fairly balmy for a spring night, and still—

All I wanted was to be in his arms again.

"God, Fall. I've missed you."

My nose stung at his admission. No, he couldn't do that. He couldn't go and be all sweet when my shields were down like this. Because the truth was, they *were* down. After tonight, after all the emotional energy even just being in this place took out of me, I couldn't hold them up any longer. Not when I was with Rafe.

I just nodded in return, swallowing hard. I didn't trust my voice, and I wasn't sure I could have admitted that I missed him even if my throat was working.

"Come on, let's get you cleaned up."

I nodded again. I might survive this evening if only he didn't require any actual human words from me. He took my hand and pulled me towards the lake. I was too busy reveling in the place where his skin made contact with mine to resist. Even through the paint, I could feel the tingles lighting me up like a sparkler in my hand.

The water was cold, it felt freezing even though I knew it was far from it. It was mild out, maybe seventy degrees. Rafe was still gentle as he pulled me into the lake after him, walking in first like he always liked to do so he could make sure the ground was steady for me.

What he didn't know was that the ground was always unsteady when he was around.

Especially now, considering that we used to—

"Remember when we used to do this?" Rafe asked, echoing the same thought I'd been having.

"Yes," I managed to squeak out. Did he think I could forget? We'd only gone out to the lake a few times. Not this particular lake, but one just outside Darlington.

It was secluded, on some land adjacent to the acreage Rafe's family owned. We had to jump a fence to get to it, but the trespassing only added to the excitement. Every moment with Rafe felt like an adventure, something out of a storybook.

Especially the night he'd first stripped off his shirt and then run down the dock and dived into the lake. He'd disappeared underneath the water, black in the night with only the moon overhead. He disappeared under so long I'd started to get worried.

But then he popped back up, his shorts in hand. He tossed them back up on the dock and then swam backwards, taunting me.

"Dare you," was all he'd said. He'd grinned at me then, that wicked, rakish grin that was so Rafe.

The boy from the past and the man from the present blended together in front of me as Rafe waded into the dark water.

There was enough ambient light out from the stars and moon to see him immediately begin to struggle out of his tux. He didn't throw the clothes back out, he just pushed them toward shore. I smiled and bit my bottom lip. Mama H would have his head for losing those expensive clothes if they just sunk to the bottom of the lake. Not that she'd chastise Rafe too much. He'd always been one of her favorites. She was a sucker for an outcast, and the secret that few had been able to see was that Rafe was always just as much of an outcast as me, no matter how many friends he had at school.

Because at the end of every day, he had to go back to that cold, unfriendly place. His house. To that family. Where he might as well have been the haint, for all the attention anyone ever paid him.

In front of me, he swam closer, water droplets streaming down his now bare chest.

My stomach clenched at the sight. Jesus, did he have any idea what he did to me? Was this all intentional? Or was he just remembering the good times, too?

I hesitated, not having ventured far from the shoreline, but then he waved me in. "Come on, we need to get that paint off you."

Oh, right. We'd come to the lake for a practical purpose. They probably didn't want the blue paint going down the drain into their septic system. After all, what if it stained the antique, porcelain clawfoot tub? We couldn't have that, could we?

I hurried into the water, feeling silly for hesitating so long at the shore. It was foolish to get lost in the past. I thought I'd put it behind me a long time ago.

The cold water on my body instantly shocked me all the way awake, out of the last of my orgasmic haze from earlier.

God, that was dangerous. He could take me so high I didn't want to come back to earth. But I had to, because I have a plan. A plan that was very important, to get everything that I—

He swam closer once I was in up to my chest. "Here, I'll help."

Then, before I could stop him, he'd begun to rub my back, massaging the paint off my skin. Some of it was dry and flaky, but some was still wet. Combined with the water of the lake, it turned into a sort of blue mud. It covered Rafe's hands as he continued to wash me.

He moved around from my back to my front, massaging my shoulder as he went.

I'd just been floating there, kind of stunned and moving my hands in the water as if I was treading it even though I was still firmly on solid ground. The sandy bottom of the lake was only a little bit rocky. I was able to stand with ease.

Rafe's hand crept around to the underside of my breast and about a thousand different alarms went off throughout my body. They were good alarms. Spasms and bright light and electricity sparking up and down my body, back and forth from wherever his hand was, straight down to my cunt.

I squirmed in the water and then finally swam away from him. All that was left was the blue paint covering my chest and my, and my—

I glanced down into the dark water but couldn't

see much of myself. I couldn't see my pussy covered with the evidence of their pawing. I did manage to stay strong for the actual Trial, but I could only handle so much.

As I swam away, I reached down and began to wash myself. When I felt clean—the freezing cold water helped the illusion—I moved on to my breasts.

A little devil sat on my shoulder, though. Because instead of keeping my back turned to Rafe, I flipped around so that he could see me. Well, see as much as he could in the dark. How well had his eyes adjusted? Could he just make out the outline of me, or not even that? If he could see the outline, could he see the way that I plucked my nipple as I washed the paint away?

From the way he froze and suddenly dipped downwards in the lake, like he'd forgotten to paddle, I thought that maybe he could see me. Or he had a very good imagination.

I knew what I ought to do. I knew what a smart woman would do.

A smart woman would stomp out of this water, grab something to cover herself even if it was only his soaked tux jacket floating near the shore of the lake, and get her ass home before she stirred up any trouble.

Back in high school, it was what I eventually

learned. Do the smart thing. Don't engage. Don't try to stand up for myself. Don't go after what I really wanted.

Just survive.

My previous record of solid A's plunged to a C+ because of the mid-semester transfer. Anyone with half a brain would have realized that it was all but impossible to catch up on those classes with so little time left.

Not my guidance counselor. She just looked at me sideways with this fake empathetic expression in her eyes as she told me she was sorry, there was nothing they could do to accommodate or help me, and I better just work harder because the school was, according to her, just "more academically rigorous" than my previous school and that was why I'd had trouble adjusting.

She wouldn't hear a word about how Becca's best friend Bree had yanked my World History paper and thrown it in the trash after I'd left the classroom after I'd dropped it off so that I'd almost failed the class. Because, of course, the teacher didn't believe me when I said, no, I had turned it in on time. I started handing my work directly to the teacher after that, but it didn't always matter. Like I said, Becca's daddy was the president of the Board, and what Becca wanted, Becca got.

When Becca didn't like that I was in her

English Class and didn't always bow or kowtow to her presence, the teacher was aware. She'd cause trouble for me and make sure I was the one who ended up in hot water, and my grade suffered because of it. That teacher played politics, and he knew who to show favoritism to. So, no matter what I turned in that class, be it a multi-faceted reading of Gabriel Garcia Marquez' *Hundred Years of Solitude* that I worked every night straight on for two weeks—it always came back with a big, fat failing grade.

On that one, the note stated it was obvious I hadn't written the paper myself, so he'd failed me. When I tried to appeal it to the principal, he'd gotten offended and accused me of trying to "pull one over" on them, and I got detention on top of it.

"Where'd you go after you left?" Rafe asked, in water only a few feet away from me. "Mom said you'd gotten a great offer to go to some boarding school that would give you an edge up on getting into an Ivy League School like you always wanted. Was it everything you hoped for?"

I only just stopped myself from scoffing. "That's what your mom told you?"

He frowned at me, but I just frowned back at him. "I told you in my emails," I said, backing a little further away from him in the lake.

In one particularly cringe-worthy email, I'd

poured out my heart about how terrible it was at my new school, how mean everyone was to me, how I missed him so desperately. How I'd do anything to just hear his voice, would he please call me? I put my phone number and then slept with my phone close to me and took it to class with me even though that wasn't allowed—just on the off chance that finally this email would get through to him and he'd have pity on me and at least call me.

There was only ever silence. Never any missed calls. Mr. Collins finally saw me staring at my phone and confiscated it one class period. I was devastated, so sure that, the way my life went, that would be the one time Rafe called and I'd miss it because of that mean middle-aged bastard.

But nope. When I finally got my phone back after yet another detention and fervently turned it back on to check—

No missed calls. Just like always.

Did my emails mean so little to Rafe he didn't even remember them? Had he even read them?

"What emails?" Rafe asked, and my unshielded heart squeezed in pain.

He didn't even remember them. I turned away from him and started to swim away. I didn't care about the cold. I didn't care about how exhausted I was. I just needed to get away from him.

It always hurt so bad. Every single time. His

casual indifference.

Just like the night, a month before he lost his brother, when everything had been... well, when I still hoped for everything like a big idiot. I was still a naive little fool who hoped Cinderella really could have the prince and the happy ending.

I'd leaned in, and he'd frozen, and we'd stared at each other.

I'd prayed he'd close the distance between us. That he'd say he didn't want to be just friends anymore. I wanted him to pour out how passionate he was about me, and how he couldn't stop thinking about me and wondering what my lips would feel like—the same way I constantly obsessed over him.

But he'd stayed exactly where he was. He didn't move in. He didn't press his lips against mine. He just stared, like a deer caught in headlights. The moment became awkward. He didn't inch closer.

And I realized his heart wasn't beating a million times a minute in his chest like mine was. He wasn't dreaming of licking his tongue along the seam of my lips like I was his. He wasn't imagining ripping my clothes off and tossing them to the floor, then pinning me to his childhood twin bed where we had our books spread out, studying.

Eventually, embarrassed, I'd finally pulled away and said it was time for me to go home.

No, I wouldn't feel his lips that night. Not until the night before I was about to leave, when I said fuck it, drove my bike over to his house the second I heard about Tim, and flung myself into his arms.

He'd held me so close and buried his face in my neck. His whole body shook. I knew without him even saying anything that this was the first time he'd been allowed to even show his real feelings in that cold house of his. That his mother may have been in hysterics over losing her favorite child to such a cruel accident but that Rafe would be the strong, stoic one.

Until he was in my arms. Still, he didn't cry. He just shook and blamed it on the rain. It hadn't been raining hard that night until then, but the whole town figured that was why Timothy had gotten in the accident. Driving too fast on a notoriously slippery curve, his car had plunged over the guard rail and into the ditch below. Timothy hadn't had a seatbelt on and had ended up thrown ten feet from the car. That was the extent of the town gossip I'd heard before I'd raced over.

Rafe hadn't told me any more, he'd just held tight to me like I was a life raft and he'd sink without me.

And then, for one moment of insanity while the rain poured and the storm thundered overhead, he slammed his lips on mine.

He'd kissed *me*. After all that time, he wanted me. I'd thrown my arms around him and kissed him back with everything I had. I wanted to take his pain away, to take it into myself, to kiss him into oblivion so he might just have one second's relief from the grief that was obviously tearing him apart.

But he'd only allowed it for about twenty glorious seconds. For twenty seconds, we lost ourselves in another world. One of lips and hands and touch and skin and tongues tangling and the most perfect madness I'd ever tasted.

And then—

And then he'd ripped himself away from me, swore loudly, stumbled backwards, and ran back into the house without even a backwards glance at me.

That was the last I ever saw of Rafe Jackson. He never said another word to me until that cocktail party a month ago.

When I'd tried to come by to say goodbye before I left for boarding school, his mother had coldly informed me he didn't want to see me but that he'd said to tell me congratulations on the new school and good luck.

And the rest, well, now I suppose it was all ancient history.

Except now, even in the cold of the lake, I could

still feel the delightful sting from the way his cock had stretched me during the Trial.

If he'd been indifferent then, what about now?

"What emails, Fallon? What are you talking about?"

He started wading towards me but my heart had had enough. The venture down memory lane plus the blue haint Trial had been enough. My brittle little heart couldn't take much more. If it broke one more time, I wasn't sure there'd be enough superglue in the world to put it back together again.

"Nothing," I said, "it doesn't matter." Then I splashed him in the face as he came closer.

He still looked confused, but another look came over his face, one I was far more familiar with. It was mischievous, full of intent.

Then he disappeared beneath the water, and just like when we were younger, I felt his arms wrap around my legs. I barely had a second to grab a gulp of air before he pulled me under.

Oh, now this was war. I came back up, sputtering for air. "Rafe, God, I wasn't ready. You almost drowned me!" I shouted.

He backed away and swore. "Sorry, I thought you'd—"

But I was just fucking with him, trying to get him off-kilter. It worked. He was completely unprepared for when I launched myself at him and dunked him.

Then I screeched, giggling as he scooped my legs again, this time tossing me over his shoulder.

"Rafe!" I screeched, laughing hard. "What are you— Put me down!"

I wriggled my still-bare ass in his face, and he landed a smack on my cheek. Dear Lord, he'd never done *that* back in the day. I squirmed on his shoulder, but finally managed to dunk him again.

We kept it up, just like we used to, except now there were more dangerous brushes, touches, pinches.

My heart had never been so full even as I told myself, *see Fallon, maybe things can go back to the way they were.*

Friends. We'd be friends.

Rafe only wanted to fuck me when it was required by the Trials. The rest of the time we'd be this. Old friends who teased each other.

Good God, the past really was a long time gone. He didn't even remember the emails. I was the only one who'd probably made such a big deal of our friendship back then anyway. To him, I'd probably been a fun companion, and like I always thought, a friendly form of rebellion against his too-stifled life.

Now? Now we could be friends again.

I'd just be careful this time to keep my shields up, *always*. Rafe Jackson could never hurt me again as long as I never let him in too deep in the first place.

We were both laughing and gasping for air when it was dèjá vu. I held onto his shoulders for leverage so I didn't have to doggie paddle to stay up in the water and he'd frozen.

We stared into each other's eyes, faces inches away from one another.

Just like that night all those years ago when we were studying in his bedroom.

I didn't wait for it to get awkward this time, though. I'd learned my lesson. I just grinned at him. His eyes widened and I thought maybe his breath hitched, but no, he was probably just short of breath like me from being dunked so many times.

Well, no rest for the wicked.

Using his shoulder as leverage, I dunked him again. Right before he went down, though, he flung his arms around my waist and dragged me with him into the dark, cold water.

It rushed around us, all noise disappearing as we plunged under the surface again, warm bodies in the cold lake, clinging to one another as for just a tiny, stolen moment, the rest of the world disappeared.

9

RAFE

"Well, if we ever wondered what house arrest feels like, we know now," I said as I walked out of the bathroom in nothing but a towel after my shower.

Maybe I should be more bashful and get dressed behind closed doors, but after days of living within these four walls, we were damn near a married couple at this point. Both Montgomery and Sully had warned me that the Trials were going to be brutal, but neither one of them really told me how the 109 were going to tick by at a speed that could drive someone mad. The fucked-up situation messed with your head.

The Trials were awful, and yet... at least it got us out of this room and actually doing something. And I had to admit that Fallon handled each disturbing thing thrown our way with a courage and strength I hadn't anticipated.

"It's finally stopped raining," she said as she flipped through a magazine, appearing as bored as I felt. "Maybe we should go for a walk or something."

"Yeah, maybe we should," I said, walking to the dresser to pull out a pair of pants. "Beau started his Initiation last night. We're overlapping our time while here. Maybe we'll see him and his belle. It'll be nice to see a familiar face."

I was desperate for some actual conversation. Fallon was never the best at communication, always a little shy, but she had usually opened up with me.

But not anymore. The girl was a closed book, and no matter how hard I tried to talk to her, she always found a way to shut down the conversation if it even came close to being about her. I knew very little about her beyond what I knew from when we were kids.

She kept repeating that the past was the past, which I got, but at the same time, I wanted more. I felt she sat on so much more but didn't feel like she could share with me. The fact that I no longer was the person she could confide in, saddened me.

I had once been that man, and time had stolen it away.

"How many of you are doing the Initiation?" she asked, still looking down at the magazine, a leg casually hung over the arm of a chair, and her hair hanging in her eyes like always. She was such a beautiful mess.

"My group is six, but they put all the Initiates in clusters by age, so more are coming, and many have been before me. Out of my six, Montgomery and Sully are done. Beau just started. Emmett and Walker are next."

"You guys were always close in school," she mumbled.

"Yeah, but not like you and me," I said honestly. "You were my best friend."

She looked up from her magazine and locked eyes with me. "Yeah..."

"Anyway," I said, breaking the connection and looking toward the window to have something other than the intensity of Fallon's dark eyes to focus on, "nothing has changed for years at the Oleander. It's how the Order does it. The age of twenty-five begins the process. Firstborn sons get the honor of becoming a member and taking over the family business."

"Is that what you want?"

I almost glanced back at her but fought the urge. I didn't want her to see the truth in my eyes. "I don't have a choice. It is what it is. My father runs the business really well and has grown it. We aren't as old money as some of the other Elders, and my father has had to really work hard to keep our coffers full at times. He's taught me a lot in his own... distant... way. The world of oil is a beast, but we've figured out how to tame it. But I think he's looking forward to passing the stress off to me... but I don't really know. We don't really talk about it much."

We didn't really talk about much at all.

My father had always been a man of few words, and after Timothy died... he nearly became mute. The only time I really ever saw him talk was here at the Oleander. He'd smile, he'd laugh, he'd act like a man who wasn't broken and beaten by the Grim Reaper. He was a different man when he wore the silver cloak. He seemed... happy and content. I was envious that he could find that when I couldn't.

"But, yeah," I clarified, looking back at her with a forced grin. "I want it."

I wanted so desperately to find that happiness my father had found in the Order of the Silver Ghost. If it lurked in these halls of the manor, then I would do whatever I could to find it as well. I needed it just as much as my father did, or I very likely could get swallowed up by the darkness that knocked at my door daily.

I didn't want to become a mute like my father.

I didn't want to become a shell of a man, and I was nearly there.

So, give me the silver cloak please. Anything to make the emptiness fade.

Fallon closed her magazine—which I was pretty sure she had already read at least once if not twice—but remained sitting in the chair by the fire. Her eyes went to my chest, my arms, my abdomen, and she asked, "When did you get all those tattoos? You didn't have any in high school, and you never said anything about wanting any."

"As soon as I turned eighteen, I got the one on my chest for Tim. Just felt right and like something I needed to do."

"Strength. Love. Honor," she said softly and nodded in complete understanding. "I think he would have loved it. Knowing Tim, he would have gotten a matching one with you."

I smirked. "My mother hates them."

Fallon laughed. "I can imagine. You have them all over your body."

"An addiction," I said with a shrug. "When things got really tough, or I was in a bad mental space, getting one seemed to help. It just became a routine in a way."

She nodded again as if she understood. "I like them."

I smiled as I went to the closet to get a shirt.

"Well, that's good. Not like I can wash them off."

There was a knock on the door, and I quickly finished getting dressed so I could be the one to answer it. "I'll get it."

"Lunch?" Fallon asked. "It feels like we just had breakfast. I swear I've lost all sense of time since being here."

When I opened the door, I was happy to see an unfamiliar staff person standing before me with the items I had requested to be delivered. I quickly took them from his arms and placed them inside. "Thanks, man," I said, wishing I had cash to tip the guy, but it wasn't like I was living in a hotel where I was free to come and go and utilize an ATM.

"Who is it? What is all that?" Fallon asked as she approached the door.

"A gift to help you pass the time away," I said, opening the boxes so she could see for herself.

Pulling out an easel first, I smiled when I heard Fallon's gasp behind me.

"Is that— Oh my god!" she squealed.

I quickly opened the next box with paint brushes, and tubes of paint in every color I could think of. There was a larger box that held several different sizes of canvases as well.

"I remember how you always loved to paint," I said as I moved the materials to a spot near the fire.

"You got these for me?" She followed closely to where I began setting everything up for her. I wanted for her to have her own space, and this was near the fire as well as by the window for plenty of light.

"I think you've read every magazine in this place, and if you're feeling anything like me, then you're about to go insane with all this time on our hands."

I stopped to glance over my shoulder at her and felt a sense of pride with the huge smile on her face I knew I caused. Her happiness lit up her entire face, and it had been the first time I had seen her look like this in a very, very long time.

"Rafe... this is so thoughtful."

"I figured that with how long we'll be here, you can paint a gallery full of paintings. At least get something out of this entire experience besides just... well... money." Realizing I was turning something good into something bad, I quickly veered directions. "I figured you'd miss painting while here."

"I actually haven't been able to paint anything since I've returned to Darlington."

I stopped cold and looked at her in disbelief. "Why? You always loved it. I don't think I ever saw you without paint all over your hands."

She shrugged, but sadness flooded her eyes.

"Life. I've just been really busy and... I don't know. I've just lost parts of me, and—"

I redirected my attention back to setting up the art area, and said, "Well, then it's about time we get to finding that lost part. You need to paint. I may not know you well now... or at least the adult you... but I do know that you have a talent that shouldn't be wasted." I cast her a smile. "And what else do you have to do while sitting in this room?"

"What about you? What are you going to do while I paint?"

"Watch you," I stated simply. Our eyes caught and I knew we were both remembering the way I used to sit and watch her paint when we were in high school. I wondered if she ever did anything with art. She was always so good, and I could get lost in the way she swirled the colors on the canvas with little effort and yet a true masterpiece would come from each flick of her wrist.

"All these supplies..." she said, as she came up beside me and lifted the paints and brushes, examining them with wide eyes that sparkled in glee. "They must have cost a fortune."

"I have it to spend." Realizing that sounded pretentious and instantly wanting to take the words back, I added, "It's the least I can do since you're helping me earn my place as CEO of my family's business. I couldn't do it without you."

She picked up a paintbrush and stood before the easel the minute I had it in place. "Can I paint something *now*?"

"I was hoping you would."

Not wasting another second, Fallon dove in headfirst. I made myself comfortable in the chair she had been sitting in by the fire which gave me the perfect view of her work. I honestly could sit here all day and watch her paint. Yes, it was a gift for her, but just as much for me.

Comfort.

Familiarity.

Memories.

"Did you go to school for art?" I asked, hoping I could get a little more out of her now that she was back in her element.

"Yes."

She kept painting and said nothing more. I suppose I should have taken that as my cue to be quiet, but I was stubborn and determined to break the wall that Fallon had clearly built around her heart.

It was me. Her friend. We used to be able to tell each other anything.

Was it this place? The Trials? Was it that we had had sex and now things were just plain awkward? Yes, we had lost touch, but it wasn't like so much time had passed by that we couldn't reconnect... or at least try. Why was she acting like we were complete strangers?

I watched her squeeze haint blue onto her palette, and I instantly knew she was going to paint something reflecting the Trial we'd endured. I couldn't wait to see what she came up with.

"How long have you been back in Darlington?" I asked.

"Not long."

"Is your mom still living here?"

"Yes."

"And you're working at a catering company?"

"I was."

Jesus, it was like talking to a brick wall.

"Why is talking to you like pulling teeth?" I asked, trying to remove any annoyance in my voice.

My intention was not to fight, and I just wanted her happy, but at the same time, I had a million questions.

Not giving up, I continued. "So, what is it you get in the end? If we pass the Initiation, what was the dream you asked for?" I figured I should know since we were a team and working on this end goal together.

"Money." She started painting on the canvas, not even pausing to speak to me.

"I know money, but how much?"

"A lot."

"Come on, Fallon... is it so hard to speak to me?"

My heart physically hurt. It constricted every single time I tried but just got rejected repeatedly by her. Who was this woman before me? It wasn't this difficult with Fallon. Not the one I'd known. Never was it this hard. It's why we were such good friends. Everything was so easy with us. She got me. I got her. We were the most unlikely pairing, and yet we just worked.

She was the only person in my life who I believed truly saw me for who I was. I wasn't just a forgotten son in the shadows of his brother's bright light when it came to her. Fallon had always made me feel special and important.

But here... in the Oleander... she made me feel like how the rest of them made me feel. Like I was nothing. Invisible. Unimportant.

If that was her intent... then why?

Just as I was about the give up and stop talking all together, she finally spoke. "I appreciate this." She stopped painting and looked at me with warmth, and gratitude washed over her face. "It's been a really long time since someone has done something so nice for me."

"That's a shame. Because you deserve things like this."

She nodded very slowly as if she were lost in thought and then refocused on her art but still spoke as she painted.

"It's important to me that we pass this Initiation and not just because of the money I get," she confessed.

She took a deep breath but continued to paint as if the act gave her the courage to open up a bit. "I'm tired of always being the poor girl getting handouts and secondhand crap. I've always been a charity and I'm over that. I love my mother, but I don't want to be like her." Her jaw got firm. "I'm breaking the cycle."

I nodded but refused to speak in fear that the minute I did, she would shut down completely.

"And I know you never saw me as a charity case," she added. "You were the only one."

She painted for a few silent moments and I just sat and watched, wondering what would come out of her work. "So, this Initiation is important to the both of us. We need to make sure we don't screw this up."

"Agreed. Although I'm not going to lie. It's hard for me to see you—"

"I know," she interrupted. "But we aren't going to pass these if we keep fighting or if you allow some weird protectiveness to eat at you. I need you. And I know you need me."

"It's not *weird* protectiveness. It's my job to protect—"

"Your job?" she cut in. "Why would it be your job to protect me?"

As if the ghosts of the manor knew we were talking about the Trials, there was a light knock on the door, followed by Mrs. H.

"Another box," I said as Mrs. H placed it on the bed.

Her attention quickly turned toward Fallon painting and she clapped her hands. "Oh, I love seeing this!" Mrs. H looked at me and beamed the biggest smile. "Good job, laddie. Very good job." She moved toward the door. "I can't stay because I have to deliver another box to Beau and his belle, but good luck tonight. It looks like you won't be doing this Trial alone."

When Mrs. H left, I moved toward the box and saw a white tuxedo like the one I had first worn for the choosing of the belle. And no surprise, there was nothing in the box for Fallon to wear.

Nudity had been her attire up to this point. Sick fucks.

But I couldn't believe what *was* in the box...

How twisted were their dark imaginations? Who could come up with this shit?

Jesus, Fallon was going to lose her mind.

"What's in the box?" she asked as she gleefully

painted away, oblivious to what was about to happen tonight.

I didn't want to tell her. There was no point in having her stew over it until it was time to leave. We still had a couple of hours before the Trial tonight. She deserved some time of happiness, and I deserved to return to what would become my chair of peace and quiet as I watched her.

She paused painting and asked again. "Well? What's in store for us tonight?"

"Just keep painting," I said as I sat down, crossed my legs and settled in. "All that stuff can wait."

She stared at me with skepticism in her eyes as she nibbled the edge of her lips. But fortunately, the pull to continue with her painting was stronger than her curiosity.

"Fallon..." I began, needing to say something that had been haunting me nearly as much as the haint of Timothy haunted the Elders. "Promise me something. When this whole thing is over, you won't hate me."

She looked up from her painting with confusion in her eyes. It was momentary, and instead of answering, she went back to painting... and I let her.

10

FALLON

I was naked again. Of course I was. I'd descended the stairs naked, carrying the only other object that had been in the box with trembling fingers: a glass dildo.

It was exquisitely made, if you were into that sort of thing. Disturbingly realistic, except for its size. It was nine inches long, and while, yeah, Rafe was close, not even he was as big as this damn thing. A heavy glass ball sack hung off the end, all meticulously crafted, I had no clue how. I'd watched a show on glassblowing once, and I couldn't even begin to imagine how one would make—

My breath caught when I got to the bottom of the stairs and entered the ballroom. It was covered floor to ceiling in *mirrors*.

Rafe was immediately shuffled away from my side to one wall where a gallery of chairs had been set up. Order members sat on the thrones watching as women of all shapes and sizes were sprawled out on the settees and some just on the bare, cold marble floor.

All of them were masturbating with similar glass dildos to the one I held. The mirrors on all sides magnified every woman five times, ten times. Everywhere you looked was female flesh, writhing and gyrating.

As I approached, an Elder with a cane walking the floor smacked one woman, *hard*, on her ass.

"You are here to trap the devil with his own vanity," the Elder chastised her. "Do you think you will capture the devil himself with that fake mockery of pleasure? Do you think he cannot see through your paltry display? Either masturbate and orgasm for real or get off the floor! You have no place here."

The beautiful woman looked up with tears in her eyes and nodded eagerly. "I'll do better."

"Silence!" the Elder said, smacking her ass again. She jumped, the cane leaving a bright red mark across the back of her ass. "The only thing I want to hear out of you are the moans of your cunt being juiced around the devil's big glass cock."

She nodded obediently but the Elder wasn't done with her.

"First I want you to gag on it. Take it out of your cunt and shove it down your throat. Deep throat it like you mean it. Like you're really tempting the devil to come. How else can we trap him if we don't tempt his vanity?"

The woman pulled the glass dildo out of her pussy where she'd been shoving it in and out relentlessly and obediently started feeding it into her mouth and—Jesus Christ!—down her throat. She must've had zero gag reflex because I could see the dildo start to poke out her throat.

"That's better," the Elder said. "Now moan around it and you—" He snapped his fingers to the woman nearest her who moaned and writhed around her own glass cock shoved deep in her pussy.

The woman perked up, pausing mid-thrust of the cock deep inside her.

"Fuck her with your dildo."

The woman immediately crawled over.

"Eat her out first."

The second woman nodded and started eating out the first woman who now choked on the cock she was deep throating. As the second woman ate out the first, the Elder must have become impatient, because he yanked the huge dildo out of her hand and started ramming it up her pussy.

And then, barely pausing, he pulled some lube out of his robe, poured it over the dildo, then shoved it up her *ass*! She squealed and shouted her surprise into the other woman's pussy.

I gasped. I couldn't help it.

They expected *me* to do this shit?

And the thought that immediately followed: Who the fuck *were* these women who came here and subjected themselves to this?

Were they rejected belles like my mother and Mama H? That had me blinking even harder, imagining my mother—my *mother*—as one of these panting women on their knees. My *mother* as the woman being fucked with a glass dildo while being instructed to eat another woman out—all while the members watched and got off—

I looked back over at the gallery and found Rafe's eyes on me.

But beyond him, I saw Montgomery. Jesus, I was supposed to masturbate with this thing in front of Rafe's friends? Montgomery had his back to the room at least, sipping some amber liquid out of a tumbler, but in addition to Montgomery, there was Beau.

Good God, was Rafe's whole high school entourage going to show up now? I know Rafe had said Beau had just started his time at the mansion and we might run into him and his belle, but I hadn't imagined our first introduction would be like *this*.

I looked out on the crowd and wondered which one of the girls she was.

"You," a deep voice called out. Looking up, a jolt went through me when I realized the Elder from the sidelines was gesturing to *me*. "What are you doing just standing there? Get to pleasuring the devil's cock. Tempt him so he might be trapped by his own vanity. There's nothing he loves more than beautiful women worshipping a likeness of his most tempting asset."

There were chuckles from some of the other men, but when I caught Rafe's imploring eyes. I wasn't sure if he was imploring me to get started masturbating so the Elders wouldn't take more of an interest in me like they had the two other women or imploring me to run away from the madness altogether. I held my head higher and walked to the center of the floor where there was an empty settee.

I lay back and spread my legs.

You can do this, Fallon Perry. And I couldn't fake it, either. I was terrible at faking orgasms, and they'd immediately be able to tell. No, I'd have to really get there.

But how to do that with a roomful of men watching on? Much less the mirrors above and on all sides that reflected me back to myself.

"No closing your eyes!" an Elder snapped, followed up by the *smack* of a cane against flesh, no doubt to reinforce his statement. "You have to look the devil in the eyes to truly tempt his presence in this gathering."

Were these guys fucking nuts? I wasn't that religious, but it seemed to me like tempting the devil at all, much less trying to trap him, even if it was a sex game, seemed like playing with fire.

But I couldn't waste any more time on silly questions or thoughts like that.

I put the head of the glass dildo to the lips of my pussy. Yeouch! It was cold! I flinched but then went with it, allowing the shudder to work its way through my body.

This was a show after all. Might as well work with everything I had.

I was barely wet, and there was no way the bulbous head was making it inside my narrow channel without some warm-up. The question was, how much time would they allow me before they expected me to be moaning and creaming over the damn thing?

Probably not long.

That's right, Fallon. Be their whore. Put on a show. Just like mommy dearest probably did countless times.

How many cocks did she suck for the great privilege of continuing to be invited back to parties like this? How many of them did she fuck?

Shit, thinking about my mother was *not* helping me get off.

I tried to clear my head. *Think about sexy things. Sexy thoughts, sexy thoughts.* I looked around. There were literally a hundred reflected images of naked, writhing bodies. You'd think that some sexual fantasy would be easy to come by.

But I saw my mother in every woman's face... except...

Except when I looked in the mirror hung right above me.

It reflected me and me alone.

And I didn't have many of my mother's features. I'd always known I likely looked more like my mysterious father, whoever he was. In this moment, though, I was grateful for Mr. Mysterious Sperm Donator, because as I watched myself with the dildo probing at my own sex, I finally started to sprout moisture down there.

Fuck, it was... *hot* to see myself like this.

I'd never watched myself masturbate before.

Whenever I did it, it was usually before bed or

in the morning, underneath the covers, a little furtively, eyes clenched shut.

But now... well, I wasn't allowed any of those creature comforts.

Eyes open, completely bared, and all but forced to look at myself getting off... which was ironically *helping* me get off.

I bit my bottom lip. Could Rafe see me? Did he like what he saw? Did he wish it was his hard cock instead of this cold dildo teasing at my lips, then slowly surging forward.

I gasped at the intrusion of the glass but didn't stop.

There was no giving up or tapping out during an Oleander Manor Trial. You were in it to win it and in until the bitter end or it was all worth nothing.

And I did not plan on leaving here empty handed, no siree.

So, I watched myself, naked, a kaleidoscope of bodies writhing around me in the periphery mirrors, and my body slickened. The huge dildo slipped in a little further and I arched to meet it, unable to help the gasp that slipped out of my mouth.

Above me, the woman's forehead in the reflection crinkled in confused pleasure. It was me, both experiencing the moment and feeling apart from it.

Even as pleasure zinged between my cunt and my belly.

Holy shit, was this actually getting me off? Jesus, I wasn't perverted like this!

But hearing another smack of a cane against an ass and a corresponding woman's yelp, I started to fuck myself even more fervently with the dildo, working it a little further in each time.

A flush rose on my cheeks and sweat sprouted at my hairline. I bit my bottom lip in concentration and dropped my legs open wider to make access for the huge glass cock. I'd never taken anything so big. Whatever artist had crafted them had made them intentionally larger than any human male could manage, likely just to torture belles. To stretch us beyond anything we could have ever prepared for.

I pushed in another inch and gasped as the girth split me open, cold glass inserted so far up inside me the bulbous head was nearly bumping against my cervix.

And somehow, that was it. I began to convulse around it.

In the mirror above, I could see the huge dildo had all but disappeared inside my warm, flushed body. My legs closed around it, and that gave even more friction against my clit.

I cried out, and it wasn't quiet. But neither were

any of the women around me. This was not the time to be shy, anyway, I knew, so I went with it. Every ounce of pleasure I felt, I vocalized.

As I dragged the dildo back out of my now-soaked pussy, I groaned with the loss of it, and as I shoved it relentlessly back in, I screamed and writhed around it.

I'd hoped after I adjusted to it, it would get easier to take. But no, it was simply too big. The second and following third thrust were just as intimidating as the first time around. Thankfully, I was cumming now.

I couldn't hold it back. There was too much stimulation, both on my cunt and also for the rest of my senses. Obviously visually—everywhere, anywhere I looked—women touched themselves and, under the direction of a few wandering Elders, they touched each other.

They suckled each other's breasts and pussies. They fucked each other with dildos and sometimes the Elders fucked them.

Finally, the men from the sidelines began to filter in, claiming women as they went.

"Now that you have courted the devil," an Elder called out loudly, "he will come and claim you. Receive him into your bodies and sate his lusts."

And then Rafe was in front of me.

Thank God it was Rafe. Oh, thank God.

"Fuck them as the devil would," the Elder continued to call out instructions. "We can only purge the devil's vanity if we fully embody him. Embody the master of sin by indulging your every wicked desire. These whores are the vessels to suck the seed from your body. To purge and purify. On your knees, Devil's whores! Let the devil fuck you every way he wants and then suck the seed from his balls till you've drained him fucking *dry*."

Rafe laid his body over mine on the settee. At first, I thought it might be to cover my modesty, that he just didn't like all these men seeing me naked. Sometimes he'd been old-fashioned like that when I used to wear low-cut tops in high school. He'd asked if I had any self-respect, that wearing shirts like that only made boys ogle me and did I want that kind of attention?

But, no, as Rafe lay over top of me, I could very firmly feel his own rock-hard member, harder than glass, hard as steel.

"Fuck me, Devil," I whispered into his ear as he bent over me. His entire body shuddered on top of mine.

And then, without another word, his hands went to his belt buckle. He undid it in record time, and then, his face still buried in my neck, he impaled me with his cock.

I sucked in a breath and grasped onto his back.

I needed to anchor myself because, holy God, he was not holding back like he must have been before.

No, Rafe was not holding back anymore. I guess I wasn't the only one watching my little show. And judging by his reaction, he'd *really* liked what he'd seen.

And the thought of Rafe watching me masturbating and getting this hard and ravenous had me juicing so much I might have fucking squirted all over his massive cock that was all but splitting me open.

Had I thought Rafe wasn't as big as the glass dildo? Because now I wasn't so sure. Maybe I'd just never seen him as excited as this.

He was filling me, stretching me, and then some. With each thrust, I was sure I wouldn't be able to accommodate his girth, that I'd have to cry uncle, that I simply couldn't go on.

But with every in and out stroke, I was about to pass out with the body and soul-shaking *pleasure*. Good *God*, I didn't know it could feel *this* good.

"Rafe," I uttered his name in a guttural growl.

Finally, his face came out from my neck. Our eyes caught as he shoved in deep again, parting my flesh, making his way, staking his claim on my territory.

I'd never be the same again after this man. I

never had been, goddamn him. He'd had me from the very first day I'd met him as a lonely five-year-old and he burst into my world like black and white meeting technicolor for the first time.

I clutched him to me and buried my face in *his* neck as my pussy clenched around him, the hardest, longest orgasm of my life spasming, spasm upon spasm, riding it higher and then higher still.

He was the only man who'd ever done this to me, who ever *could*, I was convinced. Maybe he really was the devil, because he'd always tempted me beyond all reason and sanity. I'd drop everything for the chance at even a moment with him, no matter how fucked up the circumstances.

But as my orgasm peaked even higher, I knew he wasn't the devil, not really. Because as bliss overcame my body, it hit me—how could he be the devil if he made me see God, I came so hard?

Flashing lights filled the dark kitchen as I ate my midnight snack.

I had just returned from Sully's house party and had missed curfew, but luckily all were asleep. Sneaking into my large house undetected wasn't hard...

But why the flashing lights?

Cops were outside.

Shit.

Why?

I didn't have the party while my parents were out of town. That was Sully. Was it a crime attending a party? Why were the police outside?

The loud knock on the door announced their presence to not only me, but now my parents.

I opened the door and wondered how I was

going to get myself out of this one. Had they gone to Fallon's house too? Was she in trouble for attending the party with me?

"Are your parents home?" the police officer asked. His partner stood behind him, and I could see the lights of the police car were still on. Why were they still on?

"Mom!" I shouted over my shoulder towards the stairs. "Dad!" I shouted again, although it was much harder to do because the air felt as if it had just been knocked out of me.

Something was wrong and it wasn't just because I attended a high school party.

My dad was the first one down the stairs as he put on his robe mid-stride. My mother was close behind, but she walked much slower as if afraid of who was at the door.

"Mr. Jackson," the cop said.

"Yes?" My father opened the door fully, and I moved out of the way so he could master the doorway in his powerful take-charge way.

"It's about your son, Timothy Jackson," the officer said as he took a deep breath. "He's been in a fatal car accident. I'm sorry to tell you that your son didn't make it."

"This has to be a mistake," my father demanded. He shook his head. "Timothy? No. There has to be a mistake."

"Timothy! Timothy!" my mother cried out as she lunged down the stairs as if she were determined to beat the cop for spreading such a lie.

Chaos of death. Insanity of pain.

Screams. Howls of heartbreak. Agonizing cries all with the flashing lights around. A horrific soundtrack of soul-ripping torture and denial.

My father collapsed to the ground. My mother nearly fell down the stairs. I simply stood. I watched. I waited...

I waited for Timothy to walk up from behind the police officers to tell us it was all a mistake. Nothing could touch my brother. He was untouchable. He was the golden boy. He could conquer anything that came his way... even the fucking Reaper himself.

Not Tim.

Not my brother.

He couldn't be dead.

No. No. No!

We all screamed no over and over. No!

"*No!*" I screamed as I sat up in bed, dripping in sweat. I looked around in the darkness, confused.

"Rafe?" Fallon said as her hand briefly touched my shoulder. "It's just a nightmare. It's okay. I'm here. It was just a dream."

Just a dream. Just another nightmare of that night so many years ago. I ran my fingers through my damp hair, inhaling deep breaths to try to steady my heart that felt as if it were going to break free from my chest.

"Are you okay?" Fallon asked.

Okay? Was I ever going to be okay? Years of therapy to try to deal with these nightmares, and though they had gotten better, they clearly were never going to go away. I would forever hear the screams of my parents as they found out their first-born son was dead.

"Let me get you some water." Fallon got out of bed and walked toward the bathroom.

I took the time to try to steady my nerves. It was just a nightmare, and yet it wasn't. It was real. Timothy was gone. Killed in a car accident. My reality was truly this awful dream forever.

"Here," Fallon said as she handed me a glass of water. When I grabbed the glass, she took a cool wet rag and wiped it on my forehead, my face, the back of my neck. "That must have been an intense dream."

I nodded as I drank, wishing it were scotch rather than water.

She continued to wash the rag over my body, taking away all the signs of my body's reaction to my nocturnal hell. "What was it about?"

I placed the cup down on the bedside table and put my hand on the rag to stop Fallon from her mothering touch. "I'm fine. I'm used to them. It's just the same dream I've had ever since..."

"Timothy," she answered for me.

She put down the rag and crawled back into bed beside me. Replacing the rag that was on my skin with her fingertips, she began running gentle and soothing circles on my bare back.

"I relive the night we were told he died," I confessed. I had never told anyone but my therapist about this, but it didn't feel wrong telling Fallon. She had always been my confidant before... well, before my life fell apart.

"That must be awful."

"My penance I suppose."

"Penance? Why would you have to pay penance? It's not your fault your brother died."

"I could have prevented it," I admitted, realizing I had never spoken those words that I truly felt to anyone before.

"He chose to drink and get behind the wheel, Rafe. You couldn't have stopped that. It was a terrible accident. An accident where no one is truly to blame. Sure as hell not you."

Her words should soothe but they only festered the wound that was already carved into my soul. Nothing could take away the pain, the guilt and the feeling that it should have been me in the coffin rather than Tim. He should be here in the Oleander, not me.

The devil swapped us as a sick joke.

"You know what's so fucked up?" I said as I stared straight ahead into the darkness. "I can't get that night out of my mind. It haunts me. And yet, I can't remember the days following at all. It's like I completely blocked out the aftermath. It's a void, a blur. I can't remember much of anything for a long time. I think I just operated on auto-pilot or something."

Fallon's hands continued to caress my skin which now went from sweaty to chilled.

"And yet, I can't ever forget the sounds of my parents' screams. I will forever hear that," I added.

"I'm sorry," she said softly. "I wish I had been there more— I'm sorry..."

I didn't want to talk anymore. I couldn't. I had to do something to stop the screams in my head. I had to silence them.

Now.

Taking hold of Fallon's arm, I pulled her to me and into a kiss.

It was bruising, dominating, and uncontrolled.

I didn't ask. I didn't seduce. I didn't even think.

I needed to feel her lips against mine as if it were vital to keep breathing.

When my tongue danced with hers and I heard

her breath hitch, I nearly exploded. I couldn't resist. I couldn't deny.

"I need you now, Fallon. I need to feel you."

I stripped off my sweatpants and shed her of her nightclothes and panties with zero thought or hesitation.

"I need you, too," she rasped as she kissed me again with more force than the first one.

"I need it to just be you and me. No one watching. No one dictating. No canes, no chants. Just us. I just need you in the silence of this room."

"Just us," she agreed, the determination in her eyes as unrelenting as the tone of her voice. "I want only you. We're all that matters right now."

Our lips met again, a pull neither of us could resist any longer. Our hunger never satiated. Time and distance had kept us apart for too long, but our souls never parted. Her heart beat against mine as I arranged our bodies closer, and we kissed again. But this time... this time...

The single kiss had the power to bond us forever. It could make everything right again. The kiss was the cure for the nightmares. One kiss had the power to chase the ghosts away.

I wanted her in more ways than one.

I wanted her this very second... and every day from this point on.

Now. *Forever*.

I sucked her breast, then moved to the other to give it equal attention. Lowering my hand to her mound, damp with fresh arousal, I dipped a finger to her clit and applied pressure as she roused in me an overwhelming longing that had me gasping for air.

Moving from her clit, I pressed my fingers past her silky folds and pushed one, then two, digits into her sex. She forced her hips up to drive them inside her pussy even deeper.

This wasn't enough. I wanted to feel my cock stretching her as I claimed what was now mine. I wanted to feel myself in her so badly that the hunger changed who I was.

I was an animal.

I was a stalker in search of its victim.

I was a man who needed to fuck hard. I needed to fuck so hard that the nightmare wouldn't return tonight or ever again.

Not being able to hold back the fever that scorched me, I demanded, "Spread your legs wider."

"Yes," she purred as she obeyed my command.

"You want me to fuck you?" I asked as I danced my fingers inside of her core. "Say it, Fallon. Tell me what you want."

"I want you," she panted.

"Tell me you want my cock inside of you." I

wanted to hear the dirty words come from her perfect lips.

"Fuck me!" she blurted out as a moan followed her command. "I want you to fuck me hard and make me remember the feeling between my legs for days. Make me sting. Make me hurt. Fuck! Fuck me!"

"That's my good girl," I praised. "I like that filthy mouth of yours."

She appeared absolutely desperate at this point as my fingers hit a spot inside her pussy that had her gyrating uncontrollably. I could tell she needed more.

I needed more.

"Please, Rafe. Fuck me. I want to feel you in my bones."

Hungry as I was, I was prepared to give her exactly as she asked. Not being able to wait any longer, my cock pressed up against her opening, and easily slid in with the aid of her wetness. Wrapping her legs around me, she took complete control over just how deep I would be and how fast I would get there.

Balls slapping against pussy, I was so damn deep.

I had such a craving and an urge that only she could quench.

And with forceful shoves of our hips, I drove

my cock all the way in—aggressively, possessively and completely.

"Yes, yes, yes... deeper," she cried.

In and out, I thrust, deeper and deeper with each pounding action. My moans blended with hers as our bodies merged as one. She was my dutiful soldier in this dark war of lust, and her body would forever be mine to command. I had now had a taste, and my thirst would never be satiated.

Like a vampire knocking, she had opened the door and invited me in. Now it was my time to feed.

"Fucking mine," I growled as I powered into her, my muscles taut, my eyes closed in pure bliss.

"Yours. Yours," she groaned. "I've never been anyone else's but yours."

Her pussy tightened around my dick as her words turned to loud moans that echoed against the haunted walls of our room.

"I'm yours," she repeated between her orgasmic mewls.

As if I forever had needed to hear those words, a wave of electrical current that had been resting on the cliff since I first put my mouth to hers finally released. Pure carnality shook through my body as I cried out her name.

Her arms slipped around my neck, and I rested

my head on her shoulder and closed my eyes, wishing the moment could last forever.

"No more nightmares," she whispered.

"No more nightmares," I said as I kissed her again. I didn't see sweet dreams in my future, but for right now... right now there were no more nightmares.

I was painting again, for once alone in the room. It was a rarity, but when Rafe had woken up this morning, he'd been withdrawn. Maybe he felt he'd shared too much last night, let me see too much without meaning to?

Last night was so... raw. The things he'd demanded. And I'd given in to him without a second thought.

My hand trembled as I ran it over my bottom lip. When he'd demanded I tell him to fuck me... A shiver quaked down my body even at the memory.

But when he'd woken up, he'd just mumbled that he was hungry and said I should get dressed so we could go to breakfast.

After the intimacy of last night, the intensity, the raw passion, of him finally letting me in an inch, his coldness was like a splash of cold water in my face.

I told him I wasn't hungry, and he should go alone. After all, men could wander alone in the Oleander, it was only the belles who weren't allowed to leave the room unaccompanied.

Such patriarchal bullshit. Better to focus on that than the pain of what felt like his rejection. Again.

Part of me had hoped he'd argue.

He didn't. He'd just nodded and left.

And I'd sat there in front of my empty easel feeling... well, empty.

I stared at the paintings lining the walls. The one in haint blue of a woman being swallowed into the hungry earth, a hundred hands reaching out from a graveyard to drag her down.

There were plenty of others, but my eyes settled on the most recent one: colorful explosive swirls that danced on shattered shards of glass. Some shards were bright as the sun and some were dark as sin. Others were red with pulsing blood and life and on others were sets of eyes, the eyes of God and men watching, always watching. Lust and life and death.

I stared at the blank canvas before me now.

What the hell was I supposed to paint today? I couldn't paint last night. It was too personal. Too...

Flashes of feeling Rafe push inside me, taking me so roughly, without pause and without other eyes watching us—just because he'd wanted me, he'd needed me in that moment.

God, what was I supposed to do with that?

I arranged my usual base paints on my palette and dipped my medium brush into the glob of black and mixed it with white and blue until I had a moody gray.

I lifted the brush to the canvas, still not sure where I was going with it. I wasn't sure how I even felt. About last night. About anything.

In college, for a while after I'd left this place, I felt like I'd finally found myself.

I'd shed the goth make-up. I'd let the real me come out. Or at least I thought I had.

But what if that was just another mirage? Another facade I was trying on? Healthy girl, far away from her lonely mom and the tiny apartment where we'd lived with just enough money to get by but never thrive?

Living paycheck to paycheck under someone else's thumb, and now knowing it was Rafe's parents who'd been keeping me there that whole time. Wielding their power over my mother whom they considered "less than" just because they could, because she had a dangerous secret about them and their society friends. Because she knew too much and was using me to keep her in line.

But when I started sketching the outline of a woman, it felt right. I didn't paint the lines, just the shadows. It's one of the first things they teach you in art school.

Lines are just illusions. Our limited brain's way of processing a visual reality too complex for it. No, there weren't any lines in this life, just infinite shadows and occasional light.

But... my mother also chose to stay. She'd come to these parties week after week even when she knew she wouldn't win any money or a better life.

And afterwards, she stayed in town with me.

Why?

Why couldn't she have left, broken free, run away, tried to start over?

But even as I thought it, I looked at the canvas before me.

There was no black and white, didn't I know that? Hadn't art school taught me that? That wasn't how paint, or life, worked. Black darkened and gave depth and complexity to a picture. White lightened and lifted a color. So did yellow.

But it was all such a wild mix.

Rarely did I know when I started where I would finish.

Maybe my mom didn't either.

My eyes drifted to the door.

It was so easy for me to paint Rafe with one big paintbrush swath of bad guy along with his parents, too.

He didn't call or write when I left. He never tried to find me. The only reason I was in his life now was because I'd forced my way in, but even now, he didn't want me here. Maybe for a little while last night when I'd been a warm body to lose himself in to forget about his nightmares.

I frowned and my brush strokes grew firmer as I worked in the figure's eyes and brows. I dabbed my brush in the brown, pink, blue, and white to create a skin tone, then continued.

Slowly, carefully, I painted a face. The shadowed depths of a brow and two embedded shallows for eyes. I shaped a nose, the least straightforward of any face, coaxing the paint to mimic three-dimensions. I painted the dip right above my top lip, in the center right underneath my nose.

Dipping my brush back into the pink I'd made, I started to craft the outline of lips, familiar lips that I saw in the mirror every day.

And then, after a deep breath, I went back to her eyes.

I started with the iris and built up from the bottom. A swipe of dark black and brown ocher in the center of each eye. Then I went in with my detail brush to add the flecks of gold, the shine of light, the spark of life.

Then I moved back out again, shaping her expression.

She was sad.

She was lost.

She was defiant.

She would survive. She would always survive, and she would never bow down or bend to kiss their ring. Even if they only ever saw her as fit to be on her knees, scrubbing their toilets.

She was more.

"Is it a self-portrait?"

Rafe's voice from behind me almost made me scribble a black paint smear across the cheek, but I yanked back just in time.

"Jesus," I swore, spinning around to see Rafe propped in the doorway. He looked comfortable, like he'd been there awhile. I hadn't even heard him open the door.

"Stalker much?" I asked while I tried to get my thumping heartbeat back under control.

He didn't move, he just nodded back towards the painting. "You didn't answer my question. Is it you?"

I was surprised at his question. I pursed my lips and looked back to my painting, determined not to let him unnerve me. "No," I answered succinctly. "It's my mother." It was mostly the truth. Because the more I looked, the more I saw it really was an amalgam of the two of us, a shapeshifter of both our features.

I felt more than heard Rafe come further into the room. And then his warmth was behind me, his chin all but touching my shoulder.

"She's beautiful. Is this her when she was your age?"

"Something like that."

I'd only ever seen pictures of my mom at my age, of course, but Rafe was right, she had been beautiful. She still was, in her own way, of course. But she'd been stunning at my age, and I wasn't surprised they'd chosen her as a potential belle or encouraged her to stay around for the sex parties after she wasn't chosen.

And yes, it was true that I did resemble my mother even though I sometimes denied it. When I'd first seen the picture of her in her younger years, I'd done a double-take. It was like looking at a picture of myself I didn't remember taking. Some of my features were foreign to her, but it was something about the eyes that was the same.

I suppose the real truth was that this painting was of both of us, inhabiting the same space at once.

Just like we'd both briefly inhabit the Oleander Manor.

And come away from the experience changed forever, if this past month had been any indication.

My mom had come away with me in her belly.

The doctor had put a shot in my arm to prevent that from happening even before I'd been presented to Rafe along with the rest of the belles, but how else might I be changed?

I'd have money, more money than I could ever imagine if what Mama Hawthorne said. I trusted her. Maybe that was foolish.

I trusted too easily.

So then I closed up and now no one else could get in. No one could pass the endless litany of tests to prove themselves to me.

Certainly Jeoffrey couldn't, and he'd been the nicest guy I'd ever found. But not even he could penetrate the cold, iron shield that I'd built around my heart.

"She looks sad," Rafe said, still behind me so close I could feel his warm breath on my ear. "Beautiful, but sad."

I slammed my brush down on the side table and spun to look at him. "Well, maybe she has a fucking right to be sad! Maybe life fucked her over enough times that she got wiser to people trying to manipulate her and use her. Maybe she learned to finally fight for herself."

Rafe's eyes widened. "Okaaaaay," he said. "Calm down, Fallon. It's just a painting."

Just. A. Painting?

At least he realized what he'd said and raised his hands in defense. "Wait, that came out wrong. I just meant, in real life she's happy. She's got a good job and is comfortable."

I stared at him. Was he really so clueless? "And you think that makes someone happy?"

He frowned. "Well, no, of course not. But whenever I see your mom, she's happy and smiling, and is always singing to herself. She doesn't look like that anymore." He gestured to my painting. "She found peace later in life even if she didn't have it when she was young for whatever reason."

"God, you can be so dense sometimes!"

"What? What did I do now?"

"What do you think people see when they look at you?" I asked.

He looked confused, but also like he didn't like where I was going. It wasn't going to stop me. I continued. "They see a handsome, carefree guy who has the world at his feet. Are you happy, Rafe? People look at you and they'd assume you're happy. You have everything you could need. Food. Shelter."

I stepped closer to him, ignoring the wet paint on my paint smock. "Are you happy, Rafe?" But I was already shaking my head even as he stared at me like a deer in the headlights.

"We both know the answer," I whispered. "You're as lost and unhappy as she is." I nodded back towards the painting.

Rafe's brow furrowed and then his eyes got intense. "That's not your mom, is it? It's you."

I blinked. Wait, he wasn't allowed to turn this around on me.

"Why are you lost, Fallon?" He reached out and traced his large finger across my right brow. "Why are you sad?"

I yanked back. "I'm not sad." How dare he say I was sad?

I reached down, grabbed the bright red paint tube, squirted a large glob in my hand, then turned to the canvas and smeared it in a diagonal over the painting.

The oil paint was still wet, so the red smeared into the features, and what started as a clear red streak became muddied by the woman's dark sadness by the time I got to the bottom of the canvas.

Still, when I stepped back, I was satisfied. I turned back to Rafe, and I was fierce.

"I'm not sad, I'm enraged. I paint my rage

because no one will let me fucking *scream!*"
Though I did scream the last word.

Because out here at the end of this long oak-lined lane, who the fuck would hear other than Mama H, the help, and... oh yeah, the other belle and her Initiate?

It probably wouldn't be good for her to hear another woman screaming and screeching. That would have freaked me out if I'd heard that my first week here, so I shut my mouth.

I shut my mouth and reached for another canvas, my red hand leaving prints as I went.

I didn't bother with the brush this time. I squirted out large blobs of paint, of acrylic this time, and then I started painting with my fingers.

Bright yellows, oranges, and deep reds.

I wasn't sure at first what it was, but soon I realized I was painting a phoenix. A beautiful phoenix goddess rising from the ashes.

Again and again, they tried to kill her, thought they did.

But she just kept rising.

They could never keep her down, no matter how hard they tried.

I'd all but forgotten Rafe was even there until he said, "God, I wish I could do what you do. I see it now. You're screaming on canvas. It's beautiful. You always were the brave one of us."

Goddamn him.

Dagger to the heart.

I'd started painting today to forget him. To escape him. To tell myself that he was just like his parents, that any soft spot I might have witnessed last night was just an errant moment.

But when he said things like this... or did things like bringing me the paints in the first place...

Why did he keep confusing me like this?

I had everything figured out. I had my new life, a new man, a college degree...

And yet, something had drawn me back to this accursed place. Because the truth was, Rafe wasn't the only one with ghosts of the past haunting him. His just had a face—his brother.

But me? Mine was a pain without form. Like a missing limb, I could almost feel the shape of it sometimes, a lingering loss, a lingering pain from what was once so important having been violently severed.

Because it was him.

Rafe was what I'd lost. Rafe was what I missed and ached for in the middle of the night. The part of my life that had been cut out so sharply and suddenly, and I still didn't understand why, why he'd let me go, why he'd—

"You want to learn?" I asked, cutting off my troublesome thoughts. I gestured to the canvas. *Just focus on the painting, Fallon.* Dear God, could I just get the fuck out of my own head, for fucking once?

Rafe laughed in disbelief. "What? No, I can't paint." He took a few steps back as if to prove it.

Which made me twice as determined. "That's bullshit. Everyone can paint."

I put down the canvas I was working on and pulled up another one. Mama H kept me well stocked in canvases and paints now that Rafe had requested it. What an Initiate wanted, an Initiate got, after all.

"Here, we'll start with something easy. A tree. Everyone can paint a tree."

Rafe looked at me skeptically. I just rolled my eyes at him.

"Here, put your fingers in this dark paint, right here." I mixed up some brown, black, and blue, a big glob of it.

"My fingers?" Rafe sounded confused and like I was crazy.

I smiled at him. "Yes, come on, you can't tell me you've never finger painted before."

This time he rolled his eyes at me. But like a good boy, he put his big finger into the glob of paint, though he made a face as he did it. Which was funny because the Rafe I'd known back in the day never hesitated to get dirty. As kids we'd made countless mud pies in the side garden, much to my mother's consternation. She always had to clean Rafe up before Mrs. Jackson ever saw.

"Now put it on the canvas, for the base of the tree."

He hesitated. "Where?"

I laughed. "Anywhere. It doesn't have to be perfect. We'll start building up the base. Here, we'll do it together. We're building up the shadows." I dipped my first two fingers in the paint and then reached around him from behind, guiding his arm until we were both touching the canvas.

His broad back was warm against my chest, and only now did I realize just how intimate the position was. I didn't let it deter me.

"So, do I outline the tree trunk?" Rafe asked, his hand starting to move up in a straight line.

I shook my head and grabbed his wrist to stop him. "No. Just sort of dab or make little strokes. Like this." I demonstrated and he fumbled to imitate me.

"It doesn't look like a tree," he commented.

"Ye of little faith." I said with a laugh.

I led him and we filled in more dark places as I mapped out the tree in my head. "Now we'll go back in with some lighter browns and yellows. Help me mix it on the palette."

I squirted some out of the acrylic tubes and

that was when I felt his eyes on me. When I glanced up, I met the intensity of his gaze.

Close, he was so close. He dipped his fingers in and began to swirl the colors without me even instructing. My breath caught as he grabbed my wrist and said, "Show me again," tugging me towards the canvas in a way that had my body wrapping around his from behind.

Suddenly I was *very* aware of every contour of his warm body in front of mine. Of the strength in his bicep as he extended his arm toward the painting.

Wait, what was happening? How had the power dynamic shifted so suddenly? I was supposed to be the one running this show. But now, now he was—

His firm, strong fingers interlocked with mine, smearing paint as our hands extended, the painting forgotten as my breath hitched and he spun.

He crushed his lips to mine and I wound my arms around his neck.

The tension that had built between us was suddenly released in a tsunami. We were getting paint all over each other but neither of us gave a fuck. I needed him. I needed him as desperately as he'd needed me last night.

I was so lost without him. I'd been so lost as soon as I'd left this place. I'd pretended, I'd been so good at pretending. I pretended I was a whole woman, normal. I grew out my natural brown hair and stopped with the goth make-up. I told myself I'd left Darlington in my rearview and that my past didn't have to define my future.

But it was just an open wound that had never healed.

This boy, now a man, had dug himself inside me too deep.

Yes, deep. I needed him inside me deep.

I shoved my leggings down and Rafe was on the same page. He did the same with his pants and then he had me pressed up against the nearest wall.

His cock was already rock hard, and I was slick as honey. He speared me with his cock, and I groaned in satisfaction at being filled with him.

God, *yes*. This was what I'd needed, what I'd always needed. What I'd never known but always known.

I scrabbled to grab his shirt to bring him closer but then that wasn't enough. No, I needed his skin. I shoved his shirt up and then bit at his skin. Hungry for him. For every part of him.

He shouted in surprise as I dug my teeth into his chest. And then he dragged my head up and kissed me hard, devouring me back.

He fucked me long and hard, and then he

stared into my eyes with an intensity that should have scared me but didn't. He fucked me slow and deep then.

And then tears streamed down my face as the orgasm rocked me in a series of shudders and his face went taut as he emptied himself deep inside me, each of us clutching each other for dear life.

My missing piece was in place at last. With Rafe, at last, I was truly home.

13

If I could make time stand still I would. Things had felt so normal... or as normal as you could get while locked in a room, surrounded by four walls that seemed to inch closer and closer together each day, each minute, each second. Our connection—though brief—had been real.

And as we both stared at the large box on our bed, we both knew that another Trial would occur tonight. Fallon had handled each Trial with a courage I didn't know she possessed. Frankly, a courage that I needed to get through them myself. She never faltered. She never refused. She attacked each one with a vengeance. The girl even allowed the fuckers to tattoo her hip.

To tattoo her with their Order emblem!

But from what I had heard from Sully... we

were lucky it was *just* a tattoo. The Elders actually insisted on the first two belles—and the countless belles before them—to be branded with a hot iron. Fallon lucked out by it not being done to her but rather a tattoo instead. Maybe Montgomery made changes within the Order already. Maybe...

I stared down at my fresh tattoo of the sabers crossed and realized that though I had a tattoo to forever remember this Initiation, Fallon would also forever have a reminder on her hip.

And yet... she didn't complain once. She went through the steps of this grotesque dance like a well-trained dancer. If I didn't already admire her, I would now. How could you not? I simply stood in awe of this woman and truly believed she was a belle who couldn't be broken.

"The box is big," she said as we both just stared at it. "Maybe that means there is actually something for me to wear in it."

"Only one way to find out," I said as I moved to lift the lid.

Fallon was the one to pull out the white dress with wide eyes as her mouth opened. "A wedding dress?"

There was no doubt it was a wedding dress with the layers and layers of delicate lace, and hand-stitched embroidery.

She looked at me with confusion in her eyes.

"They wouldn't expect us to get married tonight would they?"

I chuckled as I rolled my eyes. "No. No way. We aren't supposed to *marry* the belles. They're just meant for—"

Fuck me.

Sometimes I didn't think before I spoke. A brief moment of pain flashed in her eyes and then she took a few steps away from me, still holding the dress to her chest.

"Yeah, us belles are just here to be fucked and hopefully broken. What an idiot I am to even think otherwise," she snapped.

"That's not what I meant. I didn't mean—"

"I get it. Belles aren't marriage material," she said with venom lacing her words.

I took a step toward her and wished for a white flag to wave. I didn't mean to upset her. "I'm sorry."

She took another step away from me and shrugged. "I'm not delusional. I know that you precious Order boys are meant for some rich bitch socialite who has been groomed to be your wife."

She looked up at me for the first time since I put my foot in my mouth. "I grew up in Darlington, remember? I know exactly how this works."

Without saying another word, she marched to the bathroom with the dress in hand and slammed the door behind her.

Picking up the white tuxedo out of the box, I started getting dressed myself. I could go and try to knock on the door, maybe grovel some, but I knew Fallon. When she was pissed, she needed time to cool down. When the woman closed up, there was no opening her at all. And right now, we both needed to focus on the Trial coming up because something told me that this one was going to push us even further than all the other Trials combined.

———

"You look beautiful in that dress," I complimented as we walked toward the ballroom.

"Good thing we aren't really getting married since it's bad luck to see the dress before the vows," she said in a biting tone she hadn't lost since I accidentally insulted her.

Regardless of how she felt toward me, or how we both felt as we walked toward an evening that no doubt would be awful, we did appear like bride and groom with her long flowing wedding dress that hugged every curve of her body, and my white tuxedo with a violet lily boutonnière breaking up the all-white.

"If I had to marry you tonight, I would," I said softly.

"Yeah, well... annulments are easy to get. So, if

we have to then we have to. Whatever it takes to pass the Trial tonight," she said, staring straight ahead.

The sound of her heels clicking on the floor, and the swooshing of her dress helped distract me from her sharp response. But still... her words stung.

"I mean that I wouldn't want to do this with anyone else but you."

"Yeah, okay," she mumbled.

"Come on, Fallon. We need to go into this room as a team. A unit. I'm sorry I misspoke. I didn't mean to piss you off, but can you please let it go? We need to be united before we face the Elders."

Rather than answering me, she simply opened the door to the ballroom and entered. Ready or not, we were going into this Trial. I just hoped this wasn't really going to be our wedding day with the bride pissed off at the groom. The thought of marrying Fallon though... fuck. I blinked a few times. I couldn't say I minded *that* idea. The thought shocked me a little. I knew my mother expected me to marry a socialite from among her circle at some point, but I'd always imagined myself as a loner. The thought of Fallon at my side, as my partner in life, though...

I expected to see all the Elders as well as members of the Order in the ballroom when we entered. Hell... part of me expected to see a room full of wedding guests and a full-on wedding party. But instead, there was only one Elder in his silver cloak.

"Rafe Jackson, Fallon Perry, follow me," the Elder announced as he led us out of the ballroom, down a hallway and to a small sitting room.

I had been in this room a couple times as a child, so I recognized the rich mahogany furniture, the gray velvet couches and chairs, and the faint smell of cigar smoke that lingered in the air. There were even fainting couches near the windows for all the women of the past who would faint due to a corset too tightly laced to allow an easy breath.

Though the room was smaller than most in the Oleander, it still held all the Elders and the members comfortably. Everyone either sat or stood with drink in hand as if tonight were any ordinary evening having cocktails with your buddies.

"Fallon Perry, follow me," the same Elder who led us into the room said.

I considered taking Fallon by the hand and insisting I go wherever she did, but knowing her mood right now toward me, I didn't think my action would be appreciated. I just had to remind myself that she was strong—much stronger than I gave her credit for—and she could handle herself.

The Elder brought her to a small coat room off

to the right of the room. I only knew it was a coat room because as boys, we would use the room as a hiding spot during hide and go seek. Pushing her inside, the Elder then locked the door with padlock after padlock. There were so many padlocks, and though I didn't like the idea of Fallon being locked away in another room, I also didn't understand the purpose for all the locks.

"Care to have a drink?" my father asked as he approached me with a glass in offering.

I took it and nodded, surprised he talked to me. Odd that as a son, I always was taken aback every time the man spoke a word to me.

"I'm proud of you, son," he complimented for the first time in my life. "I've watched you handle each Trial with a level of poise and grace that makes me proud that you're a Jackson."

Swallowing against the lump that instantly formed in the back of my throat, I barely croaked, "Thanks, Dad. That means a lot."

"I know this isn't easy. It wasn't easy for me either. But I just wanted you to know that I'm impressed, as are the other Elders. You're going to make a fine member of the Order of the Silver Ghost."

I took a drink as we stood in awkward silence before he raised his glass to me and then turned to go join the Elders. I wasn't used to such praise—any praise—and the feelings rushing through me were foreign.

Not sure what I was supposed to be doing, and not trusting that Fallon simply stood in the coat room and nothing else, I took a few steps toward the door so I could be closer. I wanted to be able to hear her if she needed me and called out.

"These are for you," an Elder said with a large silver ring full of keys that no doubt belonged to all the padlocks on the door. There had to be over twenty of them, maybe thirty.

Before I could ask what was going on and figure out what I was supposed to do with the keys, I heard a blood-curdling scream from inside the coat room. The scream was so loud, and so ear-piercing that I almost couldn't believe it came from Fallon.

"No! Get me out of here. No!" Fallon cried as she began to rattle the doorknob and then bang on the door. "Let me out! Let me out!"

My natural instinct was to charge toward the door, but I stopped mid stride when it dawned on me that I wouldn't be able to just open the door. The padlocks would make it very difficult and time consuming.

"Fallon? What's going on? Fallon?" I shouted back deciding to ask her rather than the room full of men who didn't seem the slightest bit disturbed by the howls of a woman desperate to flee the coat room.

"Rafe! Help me out of here. Get me out. Oh God. Get me out!" Her words were followed by squeals and high-pitched screams. "Oh my God they're everywhere! Everywhere!"

An Elder's voice broke through her screams and said, "There's an old Southern belief that finding a spider on your wedding dress is good luck. It can chase the bad spirits away. And since we need all the luck we can, and help in chasing the spirit of Timothy Jackson away, we added a few more spiders to the mix."

It was then that I looked down and saw hundreds of little spiders seeping from beneath the crack of the door. Hundreds were escaping, but if there were *hundreds* fleeing... how many were still inside?

More screams from Fallon answered my question.

Spiders, oh shit! Fallon had always been terrified of spiders. It had always been one of her greatest fears... and no doubt the Elders knew it.

Sick assholes that they were.

"It is up to you to save your belle," another Elder announced. "You have all the power. You have the keys. How long she suffers is in your control. Torture her or save her. Your choice."

Not being able to take the time to process the words of the sadistic men behind me, I tried to unlock the first padlock one key at a time. "I'm coming, Fallon!" I screamed at the door as I tried to steady my shaky hand. "Hold on. I'm going to get you out of there."

"They're crawling all over me! I can't get them off! There are so many! Rafe. Rafe!"

More screams. More cries. Just like the night my brother died. Haunting sounds of distress and horror. Over and over I heard her cry and scream at the door. She pounded her fists against the wood, but I knew her actions were pointless. Only I could get her out. Only me. All on me.

I got one padlock undone, but I couldn't take joy in that since there were so many still to go. Spiders began to crawl up my leg, blackening the white fabric, but I had to focus on my hands and the keys. I stomped on them but soon realized that there were too many to defeat.

"Just keep brushing them off you. You can do this, Fallon. You can do this," I tried to soothe as I worked the locks repeatedly, trying to find the matching key.

"I can't breathe! I can't breathe!"

"Yes, you can. Deep breaths. You're strong. You can handle this."

"Get me out of here! Now! Now!"

I needed to stop the screaming. I needed to make it stop.

Just like my mother's scream.

Just like my father's howl at both the devil and God.

But Fallon's cries were worse. So much worse.

"Try to calm down, Fallon. I'm working as fast as I can to free you." Part of me wanted to ask the Elders for help, demand they assist me in getting her out, but at this point only I could do this. There wasn't enough room to have more than my hands trying to work the locks anyway.

"Please, Rafe. Please get me out of here." Her screams were becoming full-on sobs. "They're in my hair! My hair!"

I was failing her. Just like I failed my brother in saving him. I couldn't do this. I couldn't do what was required.

"Hurry!" she howled, snapping me out of my self-pity. I needed to get her out of there. "I can't be in here. I can't."

I glanced down at my legs and saw they were now nearly completely covered in spiders. The white fabric marred with little specs of crawling black. I could only imagine what Fallon's white wedding dress looked like on the other side of this door.

"I'm coming! I'm coming!"

But the screams continued.

14

I was back there. Playing in the old barn.

I wasn't supposed to be playing there. But Rafe was playing with his other friends. Montgomery and Beau and the other boys.

I didn't have any friends other than Rafe. He was popular, and I was the weird girl at school who wore old, scuffed shoes and hand-me-down uniforms. The kids made fun of me for being dirty. They said I didn't take showers, but I *did*. Some mornings I didn't have time, but I always made *sure* I didn't smell. It wasn't fair they said I smelled because I *didn't*. I made sure. I made *sure*. I even put baby powder under my arms to make *sure*.

It didn't stop them from teasing. From saying I had cooties. From saying their parents kept trying to get me kicked out of school because they didn't think their children should have to go to school with "charity cases". They'd paid good money to go here and it wasn't fair that some unwashed idiot girl got to be in the same classes as they did. The *maid's* daughter.

They'd worked *hard* to give their children the advantages they did, and what had my mother done? Spread her legs for some loser and never made it to college. Not fair, they said. It was teaching their children that hard work wasn't rewarded, that you could just skip to the front of the line with no effort. Think of the *children*.

But the board didn't budge, and I was allowed to keep going to school there. That didn't stop people from having *opinions* about it, and so, naturally, did their children, because they were not quiet about their opinions.

Everyone at school hated me. Except Rafe. His friends were nice enough to me, when they weren't ignoring me.

But Rafe couldn't protect me every second of the day, and girls were cruel. Especially Julia, who had a crush on Rafe.

She'd been mean to me on the playground today and told me no one wanted me there, and I should move to Mexico where I belonged. I was confused and told her I wasn't Mexican. She just laughed and said I was so stupid I didn't even know where I came from.

But I was born in Darlington County Hospital, same as she was, and I told her so.

That was when she hit me. When I was on the ground, she told me I was stupid again.

So, when I got home from school, I ran straight here to the barn behind Rafe's house instead of going to wait out back of the kitchens like I usually did. I didn't want Mama to see the bruise on my eye.

Stupid Julia. I kicked a hay bale, wishing it was her face.

That was when it happened.

I kicked the hay bale, and then the golden hay bale started to turn black. At first I was confused, and I bent over to see what had happened.

That was when I saw. I must have disturbed a nest of spiders, because they'd all come spilling out, little tiny spiders.

I started screaming but it was like I'd been paralyzed. Maybe they'd spit some paralyzing venom at me. That was what I thought, because I literally couldn't move.

I *hated* spiders, always had, but it was never anything like this, being so close to what felt like a thousand thousand spiders, all spilling out of that tiny hole.

Down the hay bale they went, and out onto the floor and towards the sole of my boot.

Run away. I needed to run away!

But I was frozen. Just as frozen as I had been when Julia had said those horrible things and all the other girls had laughed and laughed at me. I hadn't been able to say anything back or run away or do anything but take it and fight back tears because that would've made me look even stupider, even smaller in front of those mean girls.

And the spiders came swarming closer, closer, and all I could do was scream and watch them come. They were about to get me, to swarm up my little leg, to devour me until there was nothing left, nothing left. Just like I felt after Julia and her gang finally left me alone, it felt like there was nothing left inside—

They started up my boot and up my leggings. I screamed and screamed and felt light-headed and dizzy.

Run, run! my brain screamed, but my feet were stuck, and I couldn't do a thing to save myself.

But then there was *his* voice.

"Fallon! Fall!"

Rafe.

My hero.

He swooped in right before all those spiders ate me up.

He yanked me backwards and swept all the spiders off me. He yanked off my boot and checked for spider bites. He took me up to his room and every time I said I felt another spider and felt like crying, he'd do an in depth "spider inspection" with a flashlight to assure me I was safe now.

He made everything better when I'd been sure I was a goner.

It all came back in a flood of memories.

Except this was no memory.

This was very, very real. And these weren't innocent little barn spiders I'd unearthed. There was just enough light to see the big, fat, hairy backs of the little pests.

And the terrified adrenaline of when I was a paralyzed little girl was hitting me full force. Here I was screaming again, except Rafe couldn't get to me this time.

And they were crawling up my legs. Oh God, they were on me. They were everywhere. I couldn't get away. I couldn't bat them off, if I touched them, they'd just get on my hands, and they'd bite, and they'd--

"Rafe!" I shrieked, "Rafe, help!" I hated that all I could do was scream like a girl. A pathetic, stupid girl.

But I was frozen, crying stupid useless tears, frozen, frozen while they crawled, up my legs under the dress, up the dress, up the lace, covering the white with black, covering, consuming. They'd eat me alive; I'd just be bones in a dress. Why wasn't Rafe coming, why wasn't he saving me this time?

"Rafe!" I screamed; except this time my voice was just a hiss. One of the spiders had made it onto my chest. It crawled up my neck and my voice was gone.

Oh God, it was so big. It was so big and hairy, its legs were so long.

I could barely breathe; except I was breathing too hard. I was going to pass out, my chest was moving up and down too fast.

I tried to freeze, to stop breathing, but I couldn't stop, the panicked breaths kept coming, tears squeezed out my eyes, the spider made it up my neck. It was on my face, oh God, oh God it was on my face, my face, MY FACE, it was crawling, hairy legs across my lips—

I swayed backwards, my vision going black.

"Fallon!"

Rafe exploded through the door.

His hands came to my face and he knocked the spider off my lips. I was so dizzy I barely could feel him yanking the dress off me and stomping, stomping all around us, screaming like that would scare the little monsters back.

Then he was yanking me forwards, out of the damp, terrible little room and out into the light.

A host of men stood there just watching. They'd all been there while I'd screamed for my life. The horror of that was just barely numbed by the horror of the spiders, and they were still on me, still crawling up my legs.

I came back to life, screaming and wriggling in Rafe's arms. "Get them off! Get them off me!"

"I'm trying! Stand still," Rafe said.

But I couldn't. Now that I was finally unfrozen, I couldn't stop moving. Couldn't stop twisting and smacking at my skin.

Rafe brushed his hands all over my body but I couldn't stop. I was itchy everywhere. I felt their terrible little legs everywhere. Unending. They were all over me. They were in my hair. They were crawling in my most intimate places. I hit at my vagina, I screamed, I bent in two, I tore at my hair.

"Fallon! Fallon!" Rafe screamed, holding me to him. "It's okay, you're okay now. I got them all. You're safe. They're gone. I got them all."

But I couldn't believe him. I still felt them. They were everywhere. I was frozen and he wasn't there in time and they were biting me, eating me alive, my worst nightmare. I was still locked in that room and he was still on the other side of the door. Why was I frozen? Why couldn't I move? Why the fuck couldn't I protect myself?

"Get them off! Get them off!"

"Somebody sedate her."

I just kept screaming and scratching. Rafe held my arms at my side, shushing me. "It's okay now, Fallon. They're all gone. You're safe now."

But I couldn't stop. I could still feel them.

And then one sunk its teeth in my neck and the world went dark.

"What the fuck did you just give her?" I heard Rafe shout as my body relaxed.

"She was hysterical. Now she'll sleep. Congratulations, you passed the Trial."

And then their words came true. Darkness swallowed me whole.

When I woke, I immediately jumped up in bed, my hands sweeping up and down my body.

No spiders. I breathed out, my head sinking back.

Dear God, it was over. I was safe now. I blinked, looking around, but I could barely see a thing. It was nighttime.

I checked the clock by the bedside: 3:30 am.

What the hell? It had been early evening when we'd started the Trial.

But then I remembered, shuddering. I'd been hysterical at the end. And some fucker had injected me with something. It hadn't been a spider biting me. Those fucking bastards. Instead of helping to talk me down or soothe me, they'd just knocked me out.

Movement on the bed beside me had me looking over.

Was Rafe awake, too?

But no, he was asleep. Asleep but not at rest if the way he was tossing and turning was any indication.

His brow was knotted, distress on his face. He started to shake his head. "No," he moaned. "No, Tim, no!"

My heart squeezed.

So many nightmares in this place. But I wondered how long these nightmares had tormented Rafe.

I put my hand on his shoulder, but he shook it off. "Tim, don't," he mumbled. But then he shouted. "Don't! I'm sorry!" and startled awake.

His eyes were wild and sweat poured down his forehead.

"Rafe," I called his name. "Rafe, it's okay."

Only after I said the words did I realize I was echoing what he'd said over and over to me earlier.

But just like when I'd relived my nightmare with the spiders, my words had little to no effect on Rafe.

He whipped off the sheet and got out of bed, standing with his back to me. He was breathing so hard, his back heaved up and down.

"Rafe?" I called softly. I crawled over the bed to get to his side. "Rafe, are you okay?"

"I was too late," his voice was rough.

I frowned. What did he mean? "Too late for what?"

"I couldn't get to you in time."

I shook my head. "But you saved me. You got me out."

"Not in time!" he all but shouted, ripping his hands through his hair. "Never in time!"

I drew back, not understanding his vehemence.

"I couldn't help you. They had to knock you out."

I ground my teeth. "They definitely did *not* have to do that."

He spun around. "Don't you see? I should have gotten you out before it ever got to that point. But there were so many keys, and I couldn't find the right one."

"And that was *your* fault?" I was furious. "Seems like the fault of the twisted fucks who would put us in this situation or do that to another human."

But Rafe just shook his head. And when I reached for him, he pulled away even further.

I wanted to comfort him, but he wouldn't let me. It wasn't like last time. Even if he needed me, he wasn't going to let himself have me.

"I'm going to take a shower," he said brusquely.

I tried one last time, blinking at him coyly. Because the spiders weren't that distant a memory. Didn't he see that? I still needed him, too. He could still save me. I tried to put that in my eyes too. I tried to beg him to understand.

"I could come with you," I suggested. I begged with my eyes.

But he stayed cold. "No, I'll be fine on my own." And he turned for the bathroom without another look back. The door closed behind him with a solid *thud*.

And I was left behind, bereft and alone as always.

He could leave me so easily.

He could turn it off. Just like that.

He didn't see me. Maybe he never had. He didn't see what I needed. Maybe it was his own demons, or maybe I'd just never been that important to him.

I wasn't worth chasing, and I wasn't worth staying for.

My jaw clenched, a familiar pain slicing through my chest.

I climbed out of bed and stomped across the room to my easel and my paints. They were stacking up now after more than two months cramped up in this stupid place. Painted canvases all but covered one side of the room, some drying, others stacked up already dry.

I kicked the painting Rafe and I had started to the side. I'd been treasuring the mostly blank canvas with our messy globs of paint, stupidly preserving it out of ridiculous sentimentality.

I grabbed it off the floor and grabbed a small roller, covering it with a base gray to start a completely new picture. Erasing our painting. Erasing the moment we'd connected, erasing what I'd thought it meant, because I was obviously a stupid, stupid girl. Reaching for things that weren't there and pretending Rafe was the one to come save me when he was just a broken prince too lost with his own ghosts to ever be able to love me.

I remember the sound of silence from when I was a kid. We all sat at the dinner table together as a family... if that is what you would call us. We had our assigned chair—Dad at the head of the table, and Mom on the other end.

Timothy and I sat across from each other on each side of my father and we always used nice china, expensive flatware, and always fresh flowers as the centerpiece. It was the picture of perfection. Every single night it was expected we'd have dinner as a family.

All normal on the surface.

Except what no one would know from looking in from the outside... we ate in silence. Always silence. No questions about how our day was, how school went, or how work was going. Nothing. We ate in our own worlds even though we all sat together as a family.

Our silent family. Our mute family.

And as I ate breakfast at the head of the long table, with Fallon on the end of the other side, we sat in silence.

Our silent friendship.

Our mute past and present.

It dawned on me that I was slowly morphing into my father. He had made me all I had become. He had taught me the business that I was about to take over. He had taught me how to manage my money and make it grow even as I slept at night.

And he had also taught me how to be mute with the ones I loved.

And yes... Fallon fell into the category as someone I loved. Not that I would ever be able to tell her that. My father had taught me many things, but being loving, speaking from my heart... all skills I lacked thanks to my upbringing and my role models. I lived in my own world, and when I was hurt, angry, sad, or was afraid... I just went deeper in.

The sound of forks hitting plates had a very distinct sound. And as normal as it is for me, I did hate that it was our melody today for breakfast.

And it remained like that until Mrs. H walked in.

"Good morning," she said with a cheery disposition. When she saw that we were not matching her in mood, she asked, "How are things going? You guys are getting closer to the finish line. That has to be good."

We both looked up from our food and nodded.

"How are the Trials going?" she asked, not letting us brush her off as we were doing to each other.

"Fine," Fallon said.

"Fine," I repeated.

Her eyebrow raised. "*Fine*? From what I know of the Trials, I wouldn't exactly use that word to describe them. Care to elaborate?"

"Just a lot of sex," Fallon said as she shoveled eggs into her mouth as an excuse to not have to say anything more.

"Yeah, just a bunch of sex," I parroted.

Mrs. H crossed her arms against her chest and then huffed. "I can see you're both tired. Probably even reaching your breaking point... maybe you feel you already have."

Her face softened. "Just know that you aren't the first ones to feel this way. It's hard as you get toward the end. I've seen it a hundred times. You think you're used to the trials, but they get harder. Your patience starts wearing thin, each one tests you in new ways, breaking you down more than you ever knew possible. But you both *have* to stay together as a strong team. You have a bond and connection from your past that will keep you together through this until the very end."

She walked over to Fallon and ran her palm down her hair. "I know you're both tired. I see it in your eyes. Just focus on the finish line. You're both about to get everything you want. Don't give up."

Fallon nodded slowly and looked up at her with a weak smile. I too tried to smile my assurance that all was well and we didn't need this pep talk, but I felt anything but.

I was tired. She was right. I was so fucking tired and wanted to march out of this house every single hour of the day. Yes, we were close to the end, but each minute that passed was like a damn eternity.

Clearly seeing that neither of us were up to conversation, she said, "I'll leave you two to finish your breakfast, but maybe you should get out for a bit. Go for a walk or something. Get some fresh air." She left us then, and we were alone with the sound of forks on plates.

I cleared my throat as I wiped my mouth with a napkin. "Do you want to go for a walk today? Maybe go for a swim?" We had been locked inside for several days, and I couldn't tell you the last time I had actually seen sunlight that wasn't through a pane of glass.

"Not really," she said and then took the final swallow of her orange juice. "I'd rather get back to the painting I'm working on."

I let out a breath I didn't realize I had been holding in relief. I was hoping she would decline my offer. It had been so weird between us since the spider incident, and well... I wasn't exactly sure how to rebound and find what we once had. She kept to herself. I kept to myself. It worked, and yet it was so fucking broken.

"Okay. I have some work to do anyway," I said, though I doubted that she gave much thought or care as to what I did.

Not because she was being mean or anything. She was simply lost in her work, and frankly... I didn't blame her. I actually was a bit jealous that she had a way to escape this place. She could get lost and I just had to... well... I just had to feel lost.

We spent the rest of the day in silence. She painted and I did as much work that I could for the business from my laptop. It had become our normal. Our routine.

When there was a knock on the door, followed by the butler bringing in a box, I had nearly lost all track of time. But of course—in this place—reality always came knocking.

Fallon sighed loudly. "What lovely Trial do we get to look forward to for tonight?"

I opened the box and the minute I did, I threw it across the room. "No fucking way. No. Enough is enough."

"What is it?" she asked as she walked up to the box that now laid on the ground. "Collars?" She lifted a red one and a white one out of the box and looked at me with confusion in her eyes as she placed them on top of the dresser. "*This* is what has you upset?"

"Red means you're shared with others by my choice, and white means shared by all. And there's a note that says 'Now'. They beckon and we're just expected to have you go and fuck whoever wants you." Usually there was a black collar that meant you could keep your belle to yourself. Where was the fucking black collar?

"Okay... and..."

Her nonchalance about what I just said baffled me. "*And?* Really? No fucking way am I going to allow you to be shared with all those men in the room. You might not care, but I do!"

Her eyes got cold. "The way I see it is that no matter what, I'm getting fucked by someone tonight. So what does it matter by who?"

"Fallon!" I shouted in disbelief. I nearly charged to where she stood to shake some sense into her. "You sound like a goddamn whore right now. I know you don't mean this."

"A goddamned whore," she repeated, pursing her lips and blinking hard before shrugging.

Shit, that came out wrong. But before I could take it back, she was smiling up at me, a bright, brittle smile. "Well, maybe you don't know me as well as you think you do, and you can call me whatever you want. It's a Trial. Frankly, I'd prefer one of these damn collars over being locked in a room with spiders any day."

"You don't need to do this." I ran my hand through my hair. "Hell, *I* don't need to do this."

"Yes, we do."

I shook my head. "You want money. Fine. I'll write you a check. I'll make sure you never want again. And as for the business... I don't need to take it over. My dad will allow me to keep working there, and even if he doesn't... I have skills to get a job anywhere when it comes to oil."

"Stop," she snapped.

"I mean it. I don't know why it took me this long to realize this. But we both don't have to do this. There are other ways to get what we want. And Sully didn't pass the Trials, so I wouldn't be the first. And frankly, I don't give a shit anymore as to what people think. I'm never going to live up to Timothy's memory, so I don't even know why I try."

I paused and then looked at her. "How much

money did you ask for? I might not have as much, but I can keep you comfortable."

"I don't want your fucking money!" she yelled. "I refuse to be a charity case any longer! What the fuck is wrong with your family? I've been a charity case my entire life, and it doesn't feel good. It's time I actually get the life that I should've always had. On *my* terms. I don't want someone to give it to me. I want to take it. I want to demand it. I want to get it by my terms and my actions."

"You need to let that shit go," I yelled back. "So what if you were on scholarship at Darlington Academy. Who fucking cares? You act like that was such a bad thing. You were never seen as a charity case!"

"You have no fucking idea what you're talking about. I sure as hell was seen as a charity case. And what's worse is there were strings attached. There always are."

She was all but shaking in her fury and I had no clue why as she continued ranting, "Your mother and your father saw me as the poor little maid's daughter. They hated that you were friends with me. They hated that I was around you and the house all the time. And the minute you all could get rid of me, you did! And I wasn't on a scholarship for your information. Someone *paid* my way... as a *charity* case."

"I have no idea what you're talking about. What did my parents have to do with this? We didn't get rid of you. You left. And what do you mean no scholarship? Who would pay for you to attend? I'm not following you at all. I get that you're angry. And after what we've been through lately..."

She froze, stared into my eyes for several moments. "You know what... it doesn't matter. What matters is we will pass tonight's Trial because I'm not giving up. I'm not allowing you to give up. We committed ourselves to this, and there's no turning back. And we don't have time to discuss this anymore right now."

She picked up the white collar—the *white* fucking collar—and shot daggers my way. "This isn't just about you, Rafe. Not everything is just about you."

With that, she stormed out the door with collar in hand. And just to really piss me off... she stopped right outside the hallway and stripped off all her clothes. Tossing them inside the room, she marched toward the ballroom giving me no choice but to follow behind her.

I stomped down the stairs, finishing clamping the collar around my neck as I reached the bottom step. I heard Rafe's heavy feet clamoring down the steps behind me, but he was too late. I was striding naked into the ballroom, my white collar displayed for everyone to see.

Like usual, the ballroom was filled with naked bodies, though since we'd arrived right at the start of the party, it was mainly only the women who were naked. All women were wearing white collars.

Including me.

Gulp.

What the hell had I just done?

But I lifted my head higher. I was done playing pretend with Rafe. All it ended up doing was hurting me far deeper than any of the stupid bastards could hurt me tonight.

Rafe was not my childhood best friend, my first crush, my teenage love. Not anymore. He was just a man who I was trying to reconcile with a memory. But. It. Wasn't. Him.

And it was like running at a sprint face first into a brick wall over and over again hoping for more and then having him pull away again and again. And then what he'd tried back there in the room? Trying to give me a check like I was the whore he accused me of being. I shook my head in disgust even at the memory.

He was just like his father. Throw money at the problem instead of dealing with it. He didn't like the thought of sharing me with other men, so he'd just buy me for himself or to pay off his conscience or whatever the fuck that was about.

Fuck that.

No. It was time to get back to why I'd come here in the first place. I wouldn't be beholden to anyone but myself.

I could do this all on my own.

Rafe had finally made it to the ballroom, and an Elder led him to a chair set along the center of the wall. Courtside seats. The chair was huge, wing-backed, almost like a throne. Of course it was, I smirked bitterly.

These men thought they were kings and we were just the chattel, the consorts in their harem to please them. Nothing really ever changed from ancient times to today.

In the corner, a string quartet played. Soft, sensuous music. The cellist leaned long on his bow and the note echoed hauntingly throughout the room.

And I used what power had been given to women throughout time. The power my mother had used when she must've felt like she had no other power.

I lifted my hands, and I began to sway with the low music. It was in three-fourths time, a sort of waltz in a minor key. Back and forth my hips swayed, and I imagined what I would paint afterwards.

Chaos colors, browns sung through with bright yellows and pinks and blood red fighting for the light. Defying gravity even as hands nearby began to reach for me.

First a rough grasp on my breast. Then hands grasping my ass.

In my head, I was singing colors with the violin and painting shadows with the cello.

A man's hand reached between my legs.

I stood unmoving until other men urged my legs apart, destabilizing me until I stepped wider, allowing more access to the man who now shoved a probing finger to feel around the outside of my dry cunt.

"Somebody hand me some lube. She's dry as the Mojave."

Chuckles from the men around me.

Out of the corner of my eye, I saw Rafe shoot up from his throne. I glared him down. He didn't look away once we'd locked eyes.

His face was on fire with fury and possessiveness.

I arched an eyebrow at him, stepping even wider to allow the men pouring lube on their fingers easier access.

The bright spots of color at the height of Rafe's cheeks were so far beyond red they were almost purple.

Someone below, a finger drenched with lube, finally breached my cunt, shoving inside. My mouth dropped open at the shock of it, and Rafe saw. He took a step forward, but I warned him with my glance to stay back.

Instead, I let him see, pushing one man back out of the way so Rafe had a full unobstructed view of me. All it took was imagining it was Rafe's hand below and the natural moisture that had so far been absent sprung up like a wellspring.

A grunt from below indicated someone's pleasure at my response, but I ignored them. I only had eyes for Rafe.

And then a wet, lubed up finger probed my ass at the same time I was being finger-fucked. Other hands grasped my breasts, and then someone was sucking on my nipple while still others grasped the flesh at my waist.

I looked at Rafe. He looked like a bull ready to explode.

But I also didn't miss the bulge in the front of his suit pants.

Eyes wet with emotion, a shudder of pleasure wracked my body. Tears streamed down my cheeks as the tremors continued.

"Fuck this one's hot. She's coming so hard on my hand, she's squeezing me like a fucking vise."

"Just wait till I get my cock in this tight little ass of hers. You think that cunt's squeezing you tight, you should feel back here."

One finger retreated from my backside only for two more, it felt like two different men, trying to push in my anus afterwards.

I yelped, pushed forward by the force of their intrusion.

"Fuck this, I want to feel her on my dick. Get the fuck out of my way."

Behind me, I heard the tell-tale sound of a zipper being yanked down.

And all of a sudden, I felt panicked. Wait, wait, this wasn't just fun and games anymore. Of course I'd known in the back of my head this was where it would end up. Not just fingers and teasing touches and groping.

They'd want to fuck me. More than one of them, likely.

Maybe they'd all want to fuck me, one after the other. Did they do that to Mom? How did she feel when she'd been in this same position?

The collars were a tradition and since she hadn't been chosen as a belle, she would have been at a party like this in a white collar. All the other women here were in white collars. I didn't know about the other belle, I couldn't see her. All I could imagine was my mom. Men touching her, hands and fingers and cocks all around her.

Had she welcomed their touch, or shuddered at it like I did now? Had she wanted to scream about how unfair it was? Or did she feel power in commanding their pleasure, in bringing them to their knees as she dominated them and led them around by their cocks even if only for a few moments here and there?

Was it simply about pleasure? Because the man still exploring at my pussy had found my clitoris and he knew what to do with it. Did Mom just get addicted to men who could bring her pleasure in a world full of pain and disappointment? Was this the one place she could come, throw her body to these ravenous men, get her brains fucked out, and forget in the ecstasy of pleasure for a few hours every couple of weeks?

Would I ever know or understand?

Because the second I felt the head of a bare cock brushing against my ass, I knew the answer for myself: NO.

No, for me it was a big fat NO.

I didn't want to be fucked up the ass by a stranger. I looked to the throne, to where Rafe had stood only moments before.

But he wasn't there anymore.

For a second I felt bereft.

He'd left. Again.

It was too much for him. Although I couldn't say this time I hadn't driven him away.

It was a hurricane in my head: what did I do? Let myself get fucked? Cling so hard to what I claimed I wanted—autonomy—that I allowed myself to be used like this?

It was just a body, I tried to argue back. Who cared what happened to it or how I used it? If this was what it took to get what was owed me—

But when the cock moved against my ass, closer

to my anus, my instinctual response was again so strong:

NO.

Not like this.

Whatever I did, however I succeeded or failed in life, it wouldn't be by allowing this strange man to fuck me in this moment.

I started to yank away, twisting my pelvis away from the seeking cock. But right before I could open my mouth to say the words that would free me from this Trial, from my entire time at the Oleander, suddenly the man at my back disappeared.

My mouth dropped open in surprise as I turned to look behind me. I didn't have long to register that it was Rafe pulling all the men away from me, because a second later, he was sweeping me up into his arms and carrying me out of the ballroom and back up the stairs, away from all the prying eyes and intrusive hands.

Goddamn him, he'd rescued me after all.

And I let him.

But before I could say a word to him, to thank him, to tell him I was sorry for yanking the stupid white collar out of the box, he was slamming the door behind us in the bedroom and then dropping me onto my feet.

"Rafe, I—"

He pushed me back against the wall, pressing his body against mine and caging me in. "You drive me insane, you know that? What the fuck was that, Fallon? Did you like all those men touching you? Did you like fucking torturing me like that?"

My whole body sparked to life. From his words, yes, but also from the feeling of his body pressed up against mine.

Because I was furious, but I also felt safe, and turned on, and all of that made me even more furious, even though I couldn't even begin to untangle all the things I was feeling and whether any of them were reasonable or not.

"Maybe not everything in this fucking world is about you, Rafe Jackson," I spit back.

"It is when it comes to you," he countered.

I scoffed and the color high on his sharp cheekbones went bright again.

"Goddamn you, Fallon," he said, but then he kissed me.

I kissed him back, hard, punishing his mouth, devouring and biting. I was so furious with him. I grabbed the lapels of his suitcoat and then slipped my hands inside so I could yank his stupid jacket off. Then my fingers fumbled at the goddamned little buttons on his white dress shirt. All the while licking and biting and kissing his lips.

He eventually took over for me, yanking his

shirt off over his head and exposing all his gorgeous, tan, tattoo-covered skin for me to see. I all but attacked him, grasping his pecs and then launching myself into his arms, latching my mouth onto his collarbone and sucking, then biting.

He roared and shoved me back against the wall, reaching between my legs. I was drenched for him.

He didn't waste any more time. He gave us what we both needed when he shoved down his pants and planted that glorious cock of his deep inside me.

I clenched around him, all my inner muscles flexing and locking onto his hardness. God, I *loved* how it felt when he was hard inside me. I clung to him, so hard that he groaned as he pulled out and then pushed back in.

"You're so fuckin' tight," he swore, breathing hard into my neck. When he'd impaled me up to the hilt, he sought out my lips again. He was pinning me to the wall with his weight and his cock planted so deep inside me.

I wrapped my legs around his waist.

"Fuck me, Rafe. Please." It was agonizing with him just standing still like this. I bounced on him, needing friction, needing everything from him. He was the only one who could make me feel good. He was the only one who could fill my empty places. Goddamn him, but he was *Rafe*, and no matter how hard I tried to fight it, he was the only one I wanted.

He was the only one I'd ever wanted.

I buried my hands in his hair and yanked his head back so I could kiss him deep again. He met my lips fury for fury and passion for passion.

He lunged, filling me with his cock again and again until both of us were panting and sweat poured down his temples. But he didn't stop.

He didn't stop even as an explosive orgasm tore through me. He just leaned in so that his pelvis pressed even more satisfyingly against my clit as his cock lit up some spectacular spot inside me.

"Rafe!" I screamed as I came again, harder, higher, so bright I barely remembered to keep breathing through it.

And right as the apex of light hit, Rafe plunged deep and I felt the rush of seed as he spent himself inside me.

I grasped his face in my hands and kissed the hell out of him as the last of the shudders shook through me.

Slowly, the torrent and tidal wave receded, and it was just me and Rafe.

He pressed his forehead against mine, then rolled to the side so that we were cheek to cheek, his cock still planted to the root inside me, closer than two human beings could ever be.

I'd never been more at peace.

Until Rafe decided to go and open his big fat mouth again. "I get that you don't want a check from me, so how about this. Fallon Perry, will you marry me?"

"What the fuck?" She pushed me away from her with wide eyes.

"You heard me," I said, expecting her to try to fight this, but I didn't care. She was worth fighting for. "Marry me."

"You didn't just propose to me." She shook her head. "No way would you propose to me seconds after having sex with me and all that—" She waved in the direction of the door and the downstairs beyond. "No fucking way."

"Okay, so maybe it's not the most ideal way to do so, but I mean it. Let's get married. Let's walk away from this place together hand in hand."

"You've lost your mind!" She crossed the room and spun on her heels to face me with rage in her dark eyes. "Haven't you listened to a word I've said?

I don't want your fucking money! I want my own! Money that I can control. Money that I won't lose when you decide you don't want me."

"I get it. I do."

"No, you don't," she snapped. "You've been a blue-blooded rich boy your entire life. You don't know what it feels like to be poor. You have no idea what it feels like to live your entire life in second-hand clothes and be looked upon with eyes full of pity. I've always had to *need* someone to get by, and I'm over it. From now on, I control my destiny. So, don't you dare stand there and act like you get me. You have no idea who I even am anymore. And maybe you never did."

I took a deep breath, refusing to lose my shit no matter how much she pushed. She needed me to be strong. It was damn time I truly stood there for her. For her.

"I'm not offering you a check. I'm not offering to buy you. I know how that looked, and I can see how it hurt you, but that wasn't what I intended." I took a step toward her, but she countered it by stepping backwards. "Being here with you has made me realize that we should have never been apart. Those years you left... well... they should've never happened."

She pointed at me with strands of wild hair framing her face. She never looked more beautiful, even though fury sizzled in her veins. "I left because of *you*! Or have you forgotten that?"

"Me? What are you talking about? I had nothing to do with you leaving for school."

"Don't stand there and lie to me, Rafe. I deserve better than that."

"Lie to you?" Confusion had me freezing in place. "You left for school. Why are you angry at me over that? Why am I getting the feeling that you're livid over that and blame *me*?"

She crossed her arms against her bare chest, now just realizing that she had been standing completely naked in the room. She reached for a blanket off the end of the bed and wrapped it around herself. I took her cue to get myself in a more presentable state as well since clearly we needed to discuss some shit. Some serious shit.

"Why do you think you can just keep buying me off? You and your family. It's all about money to you all," she said as she walked over to a chair and sat down. Even though her anger had subsided, and she was no longer yelling, I could still see how mad she was.

"I told you," I said as I walked to the chair across from her and sat down as well. "I shouldn't have offered you a check. I was wrong. It's just that... I saw an opportunity to fix something. I had the ability to actually fix something. Did I want to save you? Yes. Is that so bad? At least I could finally save someone. I couldn't save Timothy, but I saw a way I could with you. That was my intention."

"Why do you feel like you could have saved Timothy?" she asked. "You keep saying that his death was your fault when it wasn't."

I took a deep breath and decided I was done keeping this dark secret locked away inside of me. I needed to release it... I needed to walk through the fire of truth and hope that there was a way out on the other side. Maybe Fallon would truly hate me at the end of this, but she couldn't hate me more than I hated myself.

"He called me," I blurted. "He needed a ride home because he was shitfaced. He had left me two messages, and I didn't pick up because I was at Sully's party with you. I was having a good time, and I didn't feel like dealing with my brother's drunk ass."

Bile rolled in my gut, and I considered running to the bathroom to puke. But I knew if I didn't keep going, I wouldn't get it all out. The purge needed to happen before I couldn't function. "I just figured he'd catch a ride with another friend. I had no idea... I didn't know he'd get in the car and drive himself."

I looked at Fallon expecting to see eyes of disgust or of judgment but saw nothing of the sort.

If anything, all I saw was compassion and understanding.

"It's not your fault," she said as she got out of her chair and kneeled at my feet, grabbing my hand in hers. "You had no way of knowing he'd make the mistake of getting into his car. And that's what this was. A mistake. Just an awful mistake."

"I could have saved him," I said as my heart seemed to rip apart as I spoke the words. "I haven't told a single soul about this because I'm so fucking ashamed. I killed my brother. I destroyed my family. It was all my fault. Had I picked up my phone, he'd still be alive. But instead, I'm here trying to fill his shoes. I'm trying to be him all while his ghost haunts my ass. He should be here. Not me. I'm the second son, the second choice."

She shook her head and squeezed my hand. "You couldn't have saved him. And you sure as hell didn't kill him. It was a terrible tragedy, but it's not your fault. It was just... it was his time."

She continued to hold my hand as she rested her head on my lap. "I wish I would have known you felt this way. I wish you would have told me so I could have been there for you as you battled this guilt. You shouldn't have had to bear this on your own—not then and definitely not now."

"I wish I would have had you too. But you left. And since I'm being honest, I can admit that I was devastated when you left but tried to understand that you had to do what was best for you. And I had just proven that I wasn't the best for anyone. Frankly, the further you got away from me the better. But I was still torn apart the day you left. I had just lost my brother, and then lost my best friend too."

She lifted her head from my lap and looked at me with narrowed eyes. "But then why did you ask for me to leave and not see you again?"

"What?" Her words made no sense. "I never asked you to leave. I wouldn't have. I fucking needed you more than I ever needed anyone in my life."

She stood up, still holding the blanket around her, and began pacing the room. "Your mother... Your *mother*..."

She turned to face me. "I came to see you and your mother met me at the door. She had told me you didn't want me to be around any longer but didn't have the heart to tell me. And considering you had just lost your brother, she told me I should do the kind thing and leave you alone. You were going through enough. And since your mother was such a kind soul, she said she would continue to pay for me to go to school. Just away from here. Away from Darlington and away from you."

I stood up as shock and fury coursed through

me. "I never knew!" I shouted. "I would have never... I never said a word to my mother. I thought you just—"

"Left," she answered for me as she nodded. "Your mother always hated me. It makes sense now. This was her way to get me out of the picture. She most likely hated that your father paid my way all those years." She paused and then studied me. "But I sent you emails. Letters. Nothing. Why did you ignore me?"

I shook my head, baffled by what she was saying. "I shut down after Tim died. I barely finished out my senior year. Mom had to help with my assignments by the end when she realized I might fail and how badly that would reflect on her, so she was checking my email, emailing my teachers for me. She must have seen and..." I felt sick when I realized my mother's full treachery.

She must've deleted Fallon's emails before I'd ever seen them. I was the only son she had left, so she'd obviously decided that if she didn't have Tim, the least she could do was start to try to control my life the same way she'd always done his. She just moved on to me, even though I never could measure up. Jesus Christ, that woman was so fucked up.

"You just disappeared and never contacted me. It broke my heart. I shut down on everyone and by the time I came back up to the surface and you hadn't even *tried* to reach out, well I thought... I thought... I thought it was for the best. I never wanted you to know that I had deep feelings for you. Far greater than just best friends. And since you were gone, I knew you were in the best place. The last thing you needed was me in your life. I thought I was poison."

I ran my hands through my hair and was happy I was locked away at the Oleander. Because if I was near my mother right now, I would fucking strangle her.

"I would have never left you," she said softly. "I thought you wanted me gone. And Jesus... I had deep feelings for you too. So deep that when your mother told me to leave, it broke me. I thought I wasn't good enough for you. I was just the poor little maid's daughter they took pity on because I was the child of the Order."

"Wait...what?" Her words were like a punch to the gut. A tidal wave of confusion washed over me. "Child of the Order?"

Fallon nodded. "My mom was a belle once. A rejected belle. In fact, the Initiate was your dad, but he chose someone else. But even though she didn't get chosen, she still participated in the Trials as one of the other women. And got pregnant with me by one of the members."

"With you? Fuck! Are you telling me that my father could be your—"

"I'm not your sister, don't worry," she quickly interrupted. Hearing the words she wasn't my sister was like a splash of cold water on my fire of chaos scorching every emotion searing through me. "Mrs. H told me all of it, and she swore your father didn't sleep with anyone during his Trials but his belle. He never ever slept with my mom. But she did get pregnant, and whoever the Elder was who did it also rejected her."

"Who was the Elder?"

She shook her head. "I don't know. If it weren't for Mrs. H, I wouldn't have even known this much. She felt I needed to know the truth about my past. She helped convince me to become a belle in the first place. She said it was my birthright. I was owed this money. I was owed all my dreams to be granted by the Order. I was owed everything my father denied me by denying my existence and letting Mom be a single mother with no support. Mrs. H knew you'd choose me"—Fallon's eyes narrowed—"even though you didn't. Anyway... she felt it was time I got what both my mother and I deserved."

"So did the Order of the Silver Ghost pay for your schooling at Darlington Academy? Did your biological father?"

"No. *Your* father did."

"Mine? Why the hell would he do that?" Every word out of her mouth sounded crazier than the last. "You just said it wasn't him who got your mother pregnant."

"No, but he felt guilty for how my mother was just shut out by whoever was my real father. I guess you could say that your father was one of the good guys in that pool of evil. So, to ease his guilt for not choosing my mother or something along those lines, he hired her to work for him and agreed to pay for all of my schooling. He figured someone from the Order should step up."

"And you had no idea?"

She shook her head. "My mother kept it all secret. I'm sure she isn't proud of it. Mrs. H told me all of this right before I became a belle. I'm still processing it myself."

She rolled her eyes and sat back down in the chair she had been in. "It sure doesn't help with my not feeling worthy issues. I can tell you that. I've always felt like I wasn't good enough. And now I do even more. My own father wouldn't claim me. I was never worth getting to know. And talk about a charity case... Can't you see? I've been one my entire life!"

"Not to me," I said.

She looked up at me and locked stares. "You say

that, and yet you offered me a check. You offered to marry me just so that I was taken care of. You can *say* the words all you want, but your actions speak volumes."

"I didn't ask you to marry me because I think you're a charity case," I said, but could understand why she would think that. "Circumstances have clearly gotten in the way of us. Don't you think it's time we stop that?"

We both sat in silence. I waited for her to answer me. For her to say something... anything. Then finally in the softest voice she spoke.

"I thought you had sent me away."

I gave a slanted smile. "I thought you had left me."

"I guess we have to thank your mother for that," she said.

"I suppose we do." More silence, but then I broke the thick air with, "So what do we do now? Where do we go from here?"

There was a loud knock on the door followed by an Elder marching into the room with the rustle of the silver cloak audibly reminding us exactly where we were and what we were still expected to do.

"The Trial is not over," he declared. "You are to return to the ballroom immediately or fail the Trial and will be expected to leave the Oleander immediately."

I stood and readied myself to tell the man to go fuck himself, but the touch of Fallon's hand on my shoulder stopped me.

"We need to finish what we began," she said softly. "We don't quit. We don't let them have any more power over what we do or don't do."

Fighting back my urge to pick her up and flee this place and never look back, I nodded. This wasn't just about me. This was about her as well.

"I can't just allow them all to touch— Jesus Christ! One of those sick fucks could be your father! So many of them were touching you! They were watching! Oh my fucking god!"

She shook her head adamantly. "I've been informed that my father is not present. He's not part of these Trials."

"But still. I can't allow this anymore. I can't."

"Stop it, Rafe," she snapped. "How many times do I have to tell you you can't fix this? I'm sorry, so sorry about Tim. But you can't fix this. I got myself in it and I'll get myself out. But I would like you by my side."

She held out her hand to me.

There was nothing else to do but to take it and trust her. I would trust her, but all the while I knew I might not be able to control myself if another man touched her and it seemed to hurt her or be against her will. She might be the woman who needed to finish this on her own, but I was still the man who would want to protect her at all costs.

Even if she hated me for it. I would not let the men of this manor and the Order break her any more than they already had. But I would also do my best not to let her down. The two impulses in me seemed impossibly at odds, but I did the only thing I could.

I grasped her hand and nodded. "Together."

And with that, we walked out of the bedroom and down the stairs, hand in hand, side by side.

"There she is," one of the Elders said, a fat man with a shiny bald head. His stomach made the robe paunch out in the middle like a medieval friar's, except that he had the bottom half bunched and held back by his belt to expose his flaccid penis that slowly hardened again at the sight of me.

A lascivious smile lit his face as he made his way across the small white ballroom to where Rafe and I entered the room, men and naked women parting before us like the red sea.

The Elder began to stroke his fat little cock, rapidly and rough, like a boy just learning how to masturbate. "Get her over here, Initiate. I want to squeeze those little titties as I ass-fuck her."

More men gathered at the Elder's side, obvious

interest on their faces. More hands went to cocks. One of them grabbed a woman being fucked by another Elder, presumably a lesser one, and forced her to her knees in front of his hard dick.

She yelped a little in surprise, but the noise was quickly cut off by the Elder, a man in his fifties maybe, with salt and pepper hair.

With a startled shock, I realized I recognized him. It was Rafe's friend Walker St. Claire's father. He was a politician. And apparently at ease in this setting, because he wasted no time authoritatively shoving his cock into the woman's mouth and down her throat.

Her eyes bugged out at first as she choked a little around him. Unlike his short, fat-cocked friar friend, he was well-endowed, and she struggled to take him.

"You," Mr. St. Claire snapped to another girl. "Get in here. Suck on my balls and you." Another snap. Another girl—oh shit, it was Beau's girl, the other Belle. She looked wide-eyed as a deer in headlights as Mr. St. Claire snapped at her again when she didn't immediately move.

"Massage my prostate. Make me come like a racehorse," he barked at her.

When she was slow to obey, looking at Beau as if for instruction, Mr. St. Claire barked, "Now! I gave you a fucking instruction, girl. That's a white collar around your fucking neck so get your fingers up my ass before I decide to fuck yours and show you what a real man feels like!"

Beau didn't seem to take offense or really much notice at all. His belle had on a white collar just like I did.

Had she been fucked already by one of these men? How many times? By how many men? And Beau had just stood there and let it happen?

But... wasn't that what I was asking Rafe to do? So why did the thought of Beau just letting this happen to his belle piss me off?

I looked to the ceiling and the glittering chandelier as the wet sounds of the women slurping at Mr. St. Claire's cock and balls echoed around the room.

"Jesus, I didn't say shove your fingers up my ass," Mr. St. Claire roared, turning so violently he yanked his cock away from the other womens' servicing mouths. "I said massage my prostate."

The Bambi-eyed belle, Abby, I think her name was if I remembered right, just blinked up in shock and what looked a little like fear. Then Mr. St. Claire rolled his eyes. "Jesus Christ, Beau, maybe teach your belle some of the fucking basics of pleasuring a man. Uma, get back there and show her where a man's fucking prostate is."

Mr. St. Claire glared at Beau. "Consider this a fucking favor."

Beau just gave a mild, uninterested smirk, and raised his bourbon glass in toast. He barely seemed to register what was going on around him, like he didn't even care if he was here, and certainly barely gave a shit about what was happening to his belle. Montgomery stood beside him, his back to the naked debauchery playing out behind him.

But I didn't have any more time to take in the drama across the room, because the fat friar had made his way to me.

"Oooo, she's a ripe one, isn't she?" A slug-like tongue slipped out of the man's mouth and slicked his lip as he reached out a hand for my breast. His other hand was still on his cock, pumping away, the fat little purple head peeking out from the end of his fisted hand every other second.

I couldn't help taking a step backwards in revulsion.

But I just bumped into a different man, my ass grazing against another hard cock. It was like at a club, where a man comes up behind you and starts to grind against you—except we were both naked and his hands immediately came to my waist, running down my sides until he reached my ass cheeks, which he squeezed hard. He rammed his cock between my ass cheeks, clutching onto them and fucking his cock up and down the fleshy channel he made with my ass.

Another man's hand was on my back, pushing me over so the man fucking my ass cheeks had better access.

The next second, a sharp *smack* had me stumbling forward. The man clutching my cheeks around his cock had just spanked me, and he hadn't held back. I was sure a red handprint was already blooming.

And then it was like open season. I was surrounded by men, a crowd of them covered over me like a tide.

I looked around desperately for Rafe, but I'd been swept away from him, or him from me. Whatever had happened, he was nowhere in sight—though granted my sight was blocked by all the tall men surrounding me on all sides, their arms and hands like octopus tentacles reaching for my every crevice.

Hands on my ass, pulling my cheeks apart. Another finger probing. Fingers pinched my nipple, then twisted. I cried out even as a man pulled me to the ground.

The floor was hard, and cold, so cold on my bare back. A man's cock hung low in my face. "Suck it," came a demanding voice from above. "Suck it down your throat. Grab my balls and pull on them while you suck me dry."

But then another cock was there, too, rubbing against my breasts, a hand rapidly masturbating. "Fuck, look at her. She's so fresh. Look how she quivers. Fuck her face, Carl. Do it. Make her choke on it."

The speaker shoved the tip of his cock against my breasts every time it was freed from his hand. "Fuck her. Do it. Oh fuck, look at these pretty titties." He slapped my breast with the hand not squeezing his cock and then before I'd even fully realized what was happening, he sprayed semen all across my breasts.

Another man immediately took his place, using the previous man's semen as lubrication to fuck my breasts.

"Take it, girl. Suck it," said the other man, holding his cock to my lips. "Open up and take what Daddy has to feed you. Suck it like you mean it." His voice got rougher. "Suck it hard, suck it like it's the best cock you've ever tasted, suck it like you want me to fuck you harder than you've ever been fucked."

Somebody spat on my pussy. Then there was laughter. "Look how wet she is."

The man holding my legs leaned over and breathed on my pussy. "Don't worry, baby, I'll make it feel good for you. I'll make you squirm while we fuck you. I'll make you howl in pleasure."

He started to massage my clit and my eyes flew open, looking everywhere, looking for Rafe.

Rafe. Rafe!

Too many things were happening at once and I wasn't ready for a single one of them. There were too many hands. I didn't have a chance to decide if I was okay or not with one touch before another was intruding.

And I knew I only had moments before the real intrusion began, before one of them shoved a cock somewhere inside me, maybe more than one at a time, before they—

"STOP!" came a roar as the man massaging my pussy dropped his head to start eating me at the same time as the cock at my lips impatiently tried to push inside my mouth.

Then the men around me started lifting their heads one by one, looking behind them like there was some kind of disturbance.

I heard cries, scuffling, then another man was yanked backward and a hole opened up in the wall of men towering over me and surrounding me.

It was Rafe!

He yanked the one bending over my legs backward by his neck collar, choking the man and making his hands go to his throat. He choked and landed on his ass as he scrambled to get away from Rafe.

All I knew was the wave of relief that swept through me like a tidal wave. I didn't know what would happen next, but it wouldn't be a strange dick getting shoved in my mouth or my pussy or my ass.

It wouldn't be more foreign hands touching my most intimate places as if they had a right to it.

Thank God, thank God, thank God.

Actually... thank *Rafe*.

I reached out for him and his hand was there, just like it had been when I extended my hand to him upstairs and asked him to trust me.

Now I was trusting him, and he wasn't letting me down.

His grip was solid as he pulled me off the ground and cradled me underneath his strong arm, cuddling me underneath his shoulder.

But his gentleness with me didn't mean he was calm. No, he shook with rage. "What the fuck is wrong with all of you?" he shouted to the now silent and still ballroom. "I don't care what the fuck Mrs. Hawthorne said. She could be a *daughter* of one of you sick fucks!"

I cringed against him at the words. Jesus, is that what he actually thought? I believed Mrs. H would never put me in that situation, but maybe she didn't know the truth? Dear God, what if she'd been wrong, and one of these men—

"Actually," said Mr. St. Claire, gently pushing the two women kneeling at his feet to the side, his cock now at half-mast. He pulled his silver robe back around himself and tied it, the sheen of the fabric catching from the glittering chandelier above his head. "She's not the daughter of any man in this room."

"How do you know?" Rafe challenged, not backing down one iota. He waved around the room. "Her mother was one of these women. You all could have fucked her." Part of me was afraid for him—he was challenging one of the alphas of the Order. But I was also proud.

He stood up for me in a way no one ever had before. And as I stood wrapped in his protective arm, watching him glare at Mr. St. Claire and demand answers, I'd never felt more treasured. I'd never felt more like I was worth... well... *fighting for*. And I *really* wanted to fucking know St. Claire's answer. These men held knowledge that belonged to *me*. It wasn't fair for them to hold it back.

"Because we know," Mr. St. Claire said.

"Who is my father?" I demanded. "Tell me. I deserve to know."

Mr. St. Claire's steely eyes moved from Rafe's to me, and there they softened. He didn't look at me lasciviously like the others did, and I realized that he'd never approached me or touched me like the other men had. As if he'd almost always had a... fatherly affection for me. Oh my God, was it him? But wait, he'd said my father wasn't in the room. What the hell was going on? I was so confused.

"Your father was a member of the Order, but he is no longer," Mr. St. Claire said.

I just shook my head, my frustration boiling over. "What does that *mean*? Who is it?"

Mr. St. Claire's jaw hardened, even as his face remained compassionate. "It's not my secret to tell."

My mouth dropped open. "But it's my *father*. I have a right to know!"

Still Mr. St. Claire stayed stone-faced.

To come so far, and still not get the answers I was seeking. And then I blinked. Holy shit. Was that part of why I'd come? For my inheritance, and for Rafe if I was honest with myself. I could admit it now. It had killed me imagining him doing all the things I knew that went on here with another woman.

I was a jealous witch and I'd always wanted it to be just me. Only me. Always ever *me*.

And I'd wanted this piece, too. To know who my father was. And now to stand here, and know that these men in front of me *knew*, but they were intentionally withholding the information from me...

But then Rafe's father stepped forward, his robe also securely on. "Your father is Edward Kingston."

I blinked. Kingston? But wait, that meant...

"I'm sorry to have kept it from you, Montgomery," Rafe's father continued, looking across the room to where Montgomery stood, face stunned. "You both deserved to know earlier."

My gaze shot back and forth between the two men. Wait, WHAT? My father was... *Montgomery's father*? That meant we were—

Oh my God, I had a brother. I had a brother.

The glass of bourbon Montgomery held fell from his hand and shattered on the floor, but then he crossed the ballroom like a silver streak. He yanked the Order robe he wore off over his head as he went. Thankfully, he still wore his suit underneath it.

As soon as he got to me, he tugged me away from Rafe just far enough to gently settle his silver robe over my head to cover my nakedness. Then he crushed me to him in an embrace. His body shook.

"Holy shit," Montgomery whispered in my ear. "*Sister*. I can't believe I have a sister. I'm not an only child anymore."

Well, that was it. I was done for. A sob erupted

in my chest at his words, because it meant now I wasn't an only child either.

I'd always felt out of step, like I didn't belong. Like I was considered an interloper, less than, by all the rich, wealthy upper-class people around me. But here was Montgomery *Kingston* of all people proclaiming me as his family. Embracing me as one of his own. Claiming me in front of a room full of people.

He squeezed me tighter, then pulled back, a wide smile mixed with concern on his face. He wiped at my tears with his thumbs. He shook his head, still looking awestruck. "I can't wait to introduce you to my fianceé, Grace. She's going to love you."

Which naturally only made me bawl harder. He wasn't just claiming me in this moment. He maybe even wanted me to be a part of his life? Oh my God, it was stupid that such a little comment could have me come apart at the seams.

Montgomery kept wiping my eyes, being big-brotherly already, as Rafe rubbed my back. Tucked between Montgomery at my front and Rafe at my back, I'd never felt more protected. I knew in that moment that the two of them would do anything to protect me, even though I barely knew Montgomery. I knew what sort of man he was by his reputation and from my brief interactions with him growing up as Rafe's friend.

He was a good man.

And he was my *brother*. The thought brought a fresh rush of joy and gratitude. And then I remembered, holy shit, I had a *father* now, too.

I reached out and grasped Montgomery's hands. "What's our dad like?" I asked eagerly.

Montgomery's face immediately fell. "I'm so sorry. He's a complete asshole piece of shit. Don't get your hopes up."

I felt disappointed but then nodded. I'd always known in the back of my head that any man who didn't claim me and left my mom in the state that she'd been was likely not a great man. It was okay to have it confirmed, even though it still hurt that Mr. Kingston had never wanted any part of me. But that wasn't Montgomery's fault. I clutched Montgomery's hands tighter and smiled at him. "I can't wait to meet Grace."

Montgomery just shook his head in wonder at me again and pulled me close for another hug. Then he pulled back and stood tall, glaring out at the crowd around us. "This Trial... no"—his face flushed with anger and certainty—"this entire *Initiation*, is hereby *over*. My *sister* will endure no more. She has passed with flying colors and has earned her reward. This ends today. Right this second."

Rafe moved from behind me so that he stood by my side. He reached out and clasped my hand, standing tall. "I'll be finishing with Fallon, one way or the other. It's up to you to decide if I've passed or failed my Initiation."

Then my beloved Rafe's strong face crumpled as he looked at his father. "I'm sorry, Dad. I'm sorry I couldn't do these Trials the way you wanted me to. I couldn't stay quiet. I couldn't be the man Tim was. I'm just not him."

And then Rafe's facade really cracked, and his voice broke. "And I'm so fucking sorry for Tim. He called me that night. It's my fault. He called and asked me for a ride. But I didn't pick up. If only I'd just picked *up*. I could have saved him, but I didn't pick *up*."

Rafe's father broke from the crowd and he headed towards Rafe, the usually reserved man's face full of an emotion I'd never seen. "Oh, son, no. No, don't think that. You've carried that all these years? I knew he called you. I saw his phone logs back then. Son, he called me too that night."

"What?" Rafe all but barked.

Rafe's father had gotten to him and reached out and grabbed his son's shoulders. "I talked to him that night. I'm sorry I never told you. I'm so, so sorry. I didn't know how to talk about that night. I'm sorry, son. He was drunk. Again. I told him not to drive. He promised me he wouldn't. I offered to pick him up, but he said he was just going to sleep it off in his truck. He swore it. Son, it wouldn't have mattered if you'd picked up. He would have told you the same. Usually, he *did* sleep it off in his truck if he'd drunk too much.

"But sometimes, and I didn't realize it until after that..." His father's voice cracked. "Until after that night, that sometimes he didn't. Sometimes he drove anyway. Your brother had his troubles. I'm so sorry. But it wasn't your fault, Rafe. It wasn't your fault."

And those words were Rafe's breaking point, because he dropped his face into his father's shoulder and his back shook in a way that I knew meant he was crying. His father tugged him in and awkwardly patted his back, neither man familiar with showing emotion in front of the other.

But they were trying, and I knew I was witnessing a healing moment, for the both of them. Oh, Rafe, oh, baby. I hoped after this moment he could truly believe it deep, deep down. It *wasn't* his fault.

Even if circumstances were different, it wouldn't have been his fault. Tim was responsible for his own actions that night. Rafe had done nothing to make Tim drink and drive, and I was glad if this could finally help him believe it and know it in his soul. It would be the first step anyway.

But then, Rafe's father pulled back. His own eyes shone with tears, though. More emotion than I even knew the man could show. He looked full of pride and love for his son, and if I wasn't mistaken, his bottom lip quivered in his attempt to hold back even more.

He swallowed hard and then looked around the room, as if only now remembering he had a larger audience. He took a deep breath and stood taller. "Rafe Jackson has also passed his Initiation with flying colors. I couldn't be more proud to pass on my robes to this man or to call him son."

With that, his dad pulled off his own robe, much like Montgomery had. While he wasn't wearing a shirt, at least he still wore his suit pants, thank God.

Rafe's eyes were still wet as his father glared in defiance at anyone who might naysay him as he then settled the robe around his son. Then he held up Rafe's hand, high into the air. "The Order of the Silver Ghost welcomes its newest member, Rafe Jackson!"

All around the room, canes started stomping the white floor beneath us until the room was a roar of echoing cane pounding.

My chest flushed with warmth for Rafe. Yes, he

was a member, but more, he had his father's love, he was set free of guilt for his brother's death, and I hoped, I prayed, he had a future he could now look to where he could explore that freedom and love to its fullest.

Maybe even with me by his side, now that I was finally free, too.

And as if he'd heard my thoughts, he turned to me, and said the one thing I'd always longed to hear from him. Not that he wanted to write me a check, or marry me, or even that he was determined to protect me.

No, he said the simplest and most profound words one human can say to another: "I love you, Fallon Perry."

And then he kissed the living daylights out of me.

I kissed him back with all the joy flooding my heart.

19

I t was over. It was all over. I couldn't believe it.

But here Rafe and I were, packing up to go home. We'd passed the test. We'd won.

And I was just sitting stunned on the bed while Rafe hustled around the room gathering both of our things and stuffing them in our suitcases. He wanted out of here as soon as humanly possible.

I wasn't sure why I didn't feel the same.

Maybe because I was a daughter of this place.

I'd literally been conceived underneath this roof, regardless of the circumstances. I finally knew the *truth*. All the missing puzzle pieces were finally in place.

The picture they created wasn't pretty or neat.

But like some of my paintings with discordant colors and images that weren't immediately recognizable, my life was beautiful when seen in its fullness.

It was perfect, even.

I was perfect. Perfect in my brokenness, in my jagged edges, in my softness, in my anger and sorrow and rage, and perfect in my joy.

Right now, this very moment, looking at the man I'd always loved more than anyone else in the world—even before he was a man when we were both children—it was perfect.

"Hey." I reached out and grabbed his wrist as he reached over to get his sleep shirt he'd cast off at the bottom of the bed. "Sit with me a minute."

His eyebrows arched. "Babe, I want outta this place. The sooner the better. Before they change their minds and decide to foist some other fucked up task on us."

I gave him a puppy dog face. "Pretty please? Just for a minute? Sixty seconds, tops."

He laughed and sat down beside me. "You know I could never deny you."

His thigh was warm beside mine. I had leggings and a long t-shirt on, but I might as well have been naked for the sparks that zinged up through my stomach at the contact.

Maybe he felt something similar, because his hands immediately came up to cradle my face. He dropped his forehead against mine and his whispered breath warmed my lips. "God, I love you so much."

Fuck, I didn't know perfect before now.

I wrapped my arms around his neck. I urged his head back. "I've waited my whole life to hear you say that."

His eyebrows scrunched. "And? Am I too late?"

My heart cracked and then *smooshed*. I shook my head. "Never." Then I kissed him for all I was worth. I pulled back only to catch a breath and so I could finally tell him, "I love you, Rafe. I've always loved you. No one but you. Always you."

He crushed me to him, and likely we would have started ditching the clothes we'd just put on if there hadn't been a loud knock at the door, and without waiting barely a moment, Mrs. H then pushed in the door.

If she was surprised at finding us intertwined, she didn't look nonplussed in the least. "All right, you two. There'll be time enough for that later. I suggest you get a move on. Some of the Elders are feeling tetchy about the move you pulled, Rafe, and it'd be better if you got gone sooner rather than later."

That had Rafe immediately jumping off the bed, his hand grasping mine firmly. "Time to go, babe."

It was so dumb, but my insides totally lit up

when he called me that. I grinned like a teenager as I hopped to my feet and helped him shove the rest of our stuff in our bags.

"Here are your phones back," Mrs. H said. She handed us our phones. She winked at me and squeezed my fingers as she gave me mine. "You might want to take a minute to peek at your bank balance, lass. It's already been processed."

"Already?" My voice choked a little on the word.

She nodded, a gleam in her eye. She gave me a quick hug, then pulled back to do the same for Rafe before leaving.

Yes, I was happy for all the reconciliation between me and Rafe, plus finding out about my brother and finally getting all the answers I'd been seeking, but I was a practical girl. If my life was really going to change in the significant ways I'd always hoped for...

I clicked the bank app open, using my fingerprint to unlock it.

It was a good thing I had a good grip on the phone because—

Holy.

Shit.

I was rich.

I was a multi-millionaire.

I could comfortably buy my mom the house

she'd always deserved, big square footage, back-yard for days, garden, probably even a pool, and it would barely make a dent. I could buy her *ten* houses.

I started giggling. I couldn't help it.

"Everything you've ever hoped for?" Rafe asked.

I tried to dim my smile but couldn't. I didn't care if it made me look like a gold digger. I'd always hated that term. And the thing was, now I could meet Rafe as an equal. I didn't need his money or his charity or for him to marry me because he felt *sorry* for me.

It never would have been that way, that wasn't who he was.

But maybe *I* couldn't believe it until now. He could tell me how he felt until he was blue in the face, but until *I* believed it, it wouldn't have mattered.

But now I was free. I was powerful.

Free and powerful to claim what I'd always wanted.

But Rafe looked sad. "So, this is it, I guess," he said, looking down at the packed suitcases. "You'll go your way and I'll go another? Back to reality. Will you go back to Pasadena?"

I just laughed at that. I don't think it was inse-curity making him say it, just his attempt to not dictate to me like before when he'd offered to write me a check or asked me to marry him. He was trying, and it meant so much to me.

But I wasn't afraid anymore. "No, I don't think I'll go back to California. Not just yet. I mean, maybe some of this art would be good for a show if I can contact some galleries and find one wishing to feature me." I looked around the room at the paintings that were piled up, mostly by the door where Rafe had started gently stacking them.

I looked back into his eyes. "I just know that I want to be where you are. I've come home and I never want to leave again." I reached out and took his hands so he would know that when I said "home," I meant *him*.

A huge grin slowly split across his face. "Just you wait, babe. I'm gonna make you Mrs. Jackson sooner or later."

I laughed out loud at that and threw my arms around his neck. Just so he knew exactly how I felt about it, I hopped up and threw my legs around his waist, too, so that he was forced to support me from underneath my backside. He massaged my buttocks as he kissed me.

Well, golly, that sure felt *good*.

We were just really getting hot and heavy, Rafe pressing me against the nearest wall, when another loud *banging* came at the door. *Bang bang bang bang.*

I pulled away from Rafe with a gasp. Oh God, had Rafe been right, and this had only been a short reprieve until the sadistic games commenced again?

But then came a low, rumbling voice, "Hey, what are you doing with my little sister in there?"

Rafe looked to me and I hopped down from him and eagerly waved my hand, motioning him to let Montgomery in the door. Montgomery's face lit up the second he saw me.

"Holy shit, sis," Montgomery said. "I can't believe we didn't see it before. Look, we have the same nose!"

He grabbed me away from Rafe and pulled me into a full-body hug. I went willingly and squeezed him back as hard as I could. It was still surreal. *Brother.* I could barely wrap my head around the concept, much less the reality.

Meanwhile Rafe grabbed our bags and passed them to Montgomery. "Hey, man, will you help us carry our bags down to the car? There's something I need to do before I leave."

"For sure." Montgomery started grabbing bags. He gave me one last kiss on the forehead, noticing the phone in my hand. "Oh good." He put down the suitcases and took it from me, programming in his number. "Call us this week, I know Grace will want to meet you right away and we have so much to catch up on."

All I could do was grin back at him like an idiot and nod. Then he was out the door. I looked back at Rafe. He was smiling too, but I noticed a crease in his forehead.

"What? What is it?"

"Nothing," he said at first, pulling me in again, like he couldn't stand to not be touching me for even a moment. Then he said, "Well, that's not exactly true. I want to say goodbye to my brother before I go. He's buried up at the cemetery on the hill."

"Oh, hon," I murmured.

"It's okay," he said, pulling back, and looking into his eyes, I believed him.

"I think I'm finally ready to say goodbye. He'll always be with me, but what my dad said..." He breathed out heavily. "It's like there's been this weight on my chest all this time and it's finally lifted. And I just, well I want to say goodbye the right way finally. Without all the bullshit in the way, you know?"

I wasn't sure I could ever know or fully understand what he'd been through, but I nodded because I wanted him to know I'd always support him. Always, as long as he'd let me. And I hoped that would be a very long time indeed.

"See you down at the car. I'll be waiting."

He smiled at that. "You better be."

"Always."

He kissed me deep then, a kiss that promised a future full and bright.

EPILOGUE
BEAU RADCLIFFE

I walked over to the window to try to keep my eyes off Abilene—something I struggled to do as every hour in the Oleander ticked by at an agonizingly slow pace. I knew the only way I was going to get through these days was to stay focused on the end game. No distractions. Chicks fucked things up for me in my life, and I sure as hell wasn't going to allow this one to mess up what was the most important test ever.

The goal of the Order was to break the belle.

Not save the belle.

Not fall for the belle.

Not live happily ever with the belle.

We hadn't been in the manor long, and I already found myself struggling, which wasn't a good sign. I had questioned if I was cut out for this secret society shit, and nearly bowed out when my time came. But what would everyone think? Would my future be over? Would my family name be ruined?

No... I needed to focus on completing each and every Trial no matter what was thrown my way. Whatever was thrown *our* way.

Luckily, I saw a distraction down below my window. Rafe walked slowly toward the cemetery, and even though I knew his reason for doing so, I decided to leave our room for a quick minute and go say hello... or goodbye since I knew his Initiation was complete. Mrs. H had told me this morning that it would just be me and Abilene now, though she remained mum on the details.

"I'll be right back," I said to Abilene who read a book by the fire which I had a feeling was going to become her normal.

She looked up surprised. "Where are you going? We aren't allowed to leave the room alone."

"No," I said as I quickly put on my shoes. "*You,* as the belle, aren't supposed to leave. I'll only be a second. I'm going to go say goodbye to my buddy." I looked up and saw the news of being left alone upset her. "Don't worry. I'll only be a couple of minutes."

Not waiting for her to argue or beg to come along, I quickly left the room, jogged down the hallway, and out of the house to catch up with Rafe who was nearly at the top of the hill.

As I approached where he stood in front of a grave, I overheard him talking and decided to give him the space to say what he came to say.

"I should have come here sooner," Rafe said as he stood before Timothy's headstone. "It was guilt that kept me away. I always thought it was me who put you here, and although I still wish I had picked up that fucking phone..."

He took a deep breath and paused for several moments. "Well, I did it. I passed the Initiation. I wanted to make Dad proud, and I wanted to honor your name. I hope I did. Can you believe it? I'm a member of The Order of the Silver Ghost. I'll be wearing one of those cloaks and being part of it all."

Rafe looked down at his feet and kicked at a root before adding, "I miss you, brother. I do. But I also have some news. Fallon Perry... remember her? Yeah, well you won't believe it, but I love her." He laughed. "Yeah, you always teased me for having a crush on her back when we were kids. And you were right as much as I hate to admit that you were. Anyway... I hope to have her in my life forever, and it gives me a sort of comfort knowing you knew her and would approve. I know you would approve."

His voice hitched, and he looked up at the sky. "I fucking miss you."

"He was a good man," I said as I walked up to Rafe and put my hand on his shoulder in comfort. "I always looked up to Tim. I'm sure he would be really proud of the man you became."

Rafe nodded. "He was a good man, and I hope so. I really do hope I served his memory well." He then looked at me. "You escaped the den of vipers for a bit?"

I shrugged and put my hands in my pockets still staring at Tim's headstone. "This shit is wild. I can tell you that. Nothing Sully told me prepared me for this." I glanced at Rafe and added, "I'm happy you completed the Initiation. Congrats. I hope I can do the same."

Rafe chuckled. "You've just begun. Trust me. It gets so much worse."

"But you passed it, so that's good."

"I'm not sure how. There were times I nearly quit. Frankly, I owe a lot of it to Fallon. That girl kept me sane."

"You are so lucky to have had someone you actually know as your belle. Being locked up with a complete stranger is bizarre. It's like the worst blind date in history over and over again. I think it's harder than the actual Trials have been."

"How are you getting along with your belle?" Rafe asked.

"Okay... not like you and Fallon, but fine. She's a good fuck and a hot piece of ass, so I guess I should consider myself lucky. But when these 109 days are over, I'm moving forward and not looking back."

Rafe laughed and patted me on the shoulder blade. "You tell yourself whatever you want. There is no way in hell anyone can walk out of this place, enduring what we do for so long, and not form some sort of connection. No way. That belle in there is going to fuck with your mind and with your heart. No use fighting it."

"Your situation is different," I said. "But I'm happy for you. Let's hope the rest of us pass the Trials and not pull a Sully."

"You got this," Rafe encouraged as he turned to leave the cemetery. "I need to get going. Fallon's waiting for me."

I walked beside him, trying not to focus on the large manor before me. It reminded me of something Stephen King would write in one of his horror novels. The moment of fresh air and the break from it all made me feel normal again. Human.

"Do you want a piece of advice?" Rafe asked as we made it down the hill.

"Sure. Anything to help get past this."

"Don't be a dick." He patted my back good-heartedly and smiled. "I know you. You don't do relationships. You keep to yourself. And you can be a super dick. I say that with love, but being a dick isn't going to help you or your belle. So, don't be a dick."

I smirked, and shoved Rafe playfully. "Got it. Don't be a dick." As we got closer to the manor, I asked the question I had been wanting to ask since I left the room. "Why do we do this? I mean... why do we care? Why is the Order so important?"

"Inherited malice," Rafe said simply. "It's in our blood. No choice."

Don't stop reading yet.
The Breaking Belles series continues with
Inherited Malice (https://geni.us/InMa-EN-n)
Are you ready for Beau Radcliffe's story?

Want a **bonus scene** of a dark initiation ritual between Grace and Montgomery, the main characters from Elegant Sins (geni.us/ElSi-EN-w)? For some extra dark, extra sacrilegious sizzle, read the scene that was too dark to make it into the book.

Go to BookHip.com/WPQXMJ to get it NOW!

ALSO BY STASIA BLACK

Dark Contemporary Romances

Breaking Belles Series

Elegant Sins [https://geni.us/ElSi-EN-w]

Beautiful Lies [https://geni.us/BeLi-EN-w]

Opulent Obsession [https://geni.us/OpOb-EN-w]

Inherited Malice [https://geni.us/InMa-EN-w]

Delicate Revenge [https://geri.us/DeRe-EN-w]

Lavish Corruption

Dark Mafia Series

Innocence [https://geni.us/Innocence-EN-w]

Awakening [https://geni.us/Awakening-EN-w]

Queen of the Underworld [https://geni.us/QuOfThUn-EN-w]

The Innocence Trilogy [https://geni.us/InBx-EN-w]

Beauty and the Rose Series

Beauty's Beast [https://geni.us/BeBe-EN-w]

Beauty and the Thorns [https://geni.us/BeNThTh-EN-w]

Beauty and the Rose [https://geni.us/BeNThRo-EN-w]

Billionaire's Captive [https://geni.us/BiCa-EN-w]

LOVE SO DARK DUOLOGY

Cut So Deep [https://geni.us/CuSDe-EN-w]

Break So Soft [https://geni.us/BrSSo-EN-w]

Love So Dark [https://geni.us/LoSDa-EN-w]

STUD RANCH SERIES

The Virgin and the Beast [https://geni.us/ThViNThBe-EN-w]

Hunter [https://geni.us/Hunter-EN-w]

The Virgin Next Door [https://geni.us/ThViNeDo-EN-w]

Reece [https://geni.us/Reece-EN-w]

Jeremiah

TABOO SERIES

Daddy's Sweet Girl [https://geni.us/DaSwGi-EN-w]

Hurt So Good [https://geni.us/HuSGo-EN-w]

Taboo: a Dark Romance Boxset Collection [https://geni.us/Taboo_Bx-EN-w]

VASILIEV BRATVA SERIES

Without Remorse [https://geni.us/WiRe-EN-w]

FREEBIE

Indecent: A Taboo Proposal [https://geni.us/SBA-nw-cont-w]

SCI-FI ROMANCES

DRACI ALIEN SERIES

My Alien's Obsession [https://geni.us/MyAlOb-EN-w]

My Alien's Baby [https://geni.us/MyAlBa-EN-w]

My Alien's Beast [https://geni.us/MyAlBe-EN-w]

MARRIAGE RAFFLE SERIES

Theirs To Protect [https://geni.us/Th2Pr-EN-w]

Theirs To Pleasure [https://geni.us/Th2Pl-EN-w]

Theirs To Wed [https://geni.us/Th2We-EN-w]

Theirs To Defy [https://geni.us/Th2De-EN-w]

Theirs To Ransom [https://geni.us/Th2Ra-EN-w]

Marriage Raffle Boxset Part 1 [https://geni.us/MaRaBx-EN-w]

Marriage Raffle Boxset Part 2 [https://geni.us/MaRaBx-2-EN-w]

FREEBIE

Their Honeymoon [https://BookHip.com/QHCQDM]

ALSO BY ALTA HENSLEY

For all of my books, check out my Amazon Page!

http://amzn.to/2CTmeen

Secret Bride Series:

Captive Bride

Kept Bride

Taken Bride

Top Shelf Series:

Bastards & Whiskey

Villains & Vodka

Scoundrels & Scotch

Devils & Rye

Beasts & Bourbon

Sinners & Gin

Evil Lies Series:

The Truth About Cinder

The Truth About Alice

ABOUT STASIA BLACK

STASIA BLACK grew up in Texas, recently spent a freezing five-year stint in Minnesota, and now is happily planted in sunny California, which she will never, ever leave.

She loves writing, reading, listening to podcasts, and has recently taken up biking after a twenty-year sabbatical (and has the bumps and bruises to prove it). She lives with her own personal cheerleader, aka, her handsome husband, and their teenage son. Wow. Typing that makes her feel old. And writing about herself in the third person makes her feel a little like a nutjob, but ahem! Where were we?

Stasia's drawn to romantic stories that don't take the easy way out. She wants to see beneath people's veneer and poke into their dark places, their twisted motives, and their deepest desires. Basically, she wants to create characters that make readers alternately laugh, cry ugly tears, want to toss their kindles across the room, and then declare they have a new FBB (forever book boyfriend).

Join Stasia's Facebook Group for Readers for access to deleted scenes, to chat with me and other fans and also get access to exclusive giveaways:

Stasia's Facebook Reader Group
(facebook.com/groups/1047415562052038/)

Want to read an EXCLUSIVE, FREE novella, Indecent: a Taboo Proposal, that is available ONLY to my newsletter subscribers, along with news about upcoming releases, sales, exclusive giveaways, and more?

Get **Indecent: a Taboo Proposal**
(geni.us/SBA-nw-cont-w)

When Mia's boyfriend takes her out to her favorite restaurant on their six-year anniversary, she's expecting one kind of proposal. What she didn't expect was her boyfriend's longtime rival, Vaughn McBride, to show up and make a completely different sort of offer: all her boyfriend's debts will be wiped clear. The price?

One night with her.

Website: stasiablack.com
Facebook: facebook.com/StasiaBlackAuthor
Twitter: twitter.com/stasiawritesmut
Instagram: instagram.com/stasiablackauthor
Goodreads: goodreads.com/stasiablack
BookBub: bookbub.com/authors/stasia-black

ABOUT ALTA HENSLEY

ALTA HENSLEY is a USA TODAY bestselling
author of hot, dark and dirty romance. She is also
an Amazon Top 100 bestselling author. Being a
multi-published author in the romance
genre, Alta is known for her dark, gritty alpha
heroes, sometimes sweet love stories, hot eroticism,
and engaging tales of the constant struggle
between dominance and submission.

As a gift for being my reader, I would like to offer
you a FREE book.
DELICATE SCARS
Get your copy now! ~
https://dl.bookfunnel.com/tnpuad5675

Join Alta's Facebook Group for Readers for access

to deleted scenes, to chat with me and other fans and also get access to exclusive giveaways:
Alta's Private Facebook Room

As a gift for being my reader, I would like to offer you a FREE book.
DELICATE SCARS
Get your copy now! ~
https://dl.bookfunnel.com/tnpuad5675

Check out Alta Hensley:
Website: www.altahensley.com
Facebook: facebook.com/AltaHensleyAuthor
Twitter: twitter.com/AltaHensley
Instagram: instagram.com/altahensley
BookBub: bookbub.com/authors/alta-hensley
Sign up for Alta's Newsletter:
readerlinks.com/l/727720/nl

www.ingramcontent.com/pod-product-compliance
Lightning Source LLC
Chambersburg PA
CBHW060858250626
47159CB00008B/2785